Cheetah's Win

Phil Geusz

With special thanks to Jacob O'Hare.

Beep-beep! Beep-beep!

Why won't that jackass shut up! I thought to myself, rolling over and clamping the pillow even more firmly over my head. It was hot—damned hot!—and hard enough for a man with a pounding head to sleep without some idiot and his horn to make things even worse!

Beep-beep! Beep-beep!

Damnit! I rolled over a little more and instantly regretted the move. Something hurt like hell behind my left shoulder, and now there was bright, painful sunlight on my face. "Crap!" I declared to the world in general, trying to worm my way back under my pillow. "The whole universe is a load of crap!"

"Señor?" a young voice asked from very nearby, and suddenly I was wide, wide awake. Had I really. . .

"Señor?" the voice repeated, more urgently. "Señor?"

Beep-beep! Beep-beep!Beeeeeeeeeeeeeeeep!

Jesus Christ almighty! I really had! And when Julio stretched out his horn like that. . .

Then a big turbine engine started and I knew that I was in very deep doo-doo indeed. My eyes flew open despite the awl-stabs of pain brought on by the bright Dominican sunshine, and I sat bolt upright. "Señor!" the too-young hooker in bed next to me repeated, looking terribly worried.

"Si," I muttered, clambering to my feet and balancing as best I could on the heaving, rocking floor. My billfold was still on the nightstand; at least I'd engaged an honest prostitute. Even if she *was* a little young. Perhaps the two went together, I reasoned fuzzily. I knocked over two rum bottles, one of them not quite empty, before finally grasping my prize. The wallet still had a wad of bills inside of it; I snatched them out and threw them down on the nightstand, uncounted. "Muchos gracias, Señiorita." Then the big motor on the team bus roared out and there was no time left at all. My pants were lying right there in front of me, but even those few seconds would've been too long. Instead I raced for the door like a gazelle.

I'd always been a fast runner; fastest in my elementary school, fastest on my track team, even fastest in the Major Leagues, once upon a time. Despite being barefoot and extremely hung over I was down the stairs and halfway out the door before Julio managed to grind the team bus's balky gearbox into first. "Hold up!" I tried to scream through parched lips and arid tongue. "Hold up!" But all that came out was a pathetic little hiss.

There was an old man sitting on the hotel's porch. I vaguely remembered not having liked him very much the night before for some reason or another, so I didn't feel too bad about snatching the big Mexican-style sombrero off of his head without even slowing down and then using it to cover my privates. The man gabbled something, but it didn't matter. After all, *he'd* never been the fastest man in the bigs. So, what could he do about it? Steal a base, steal a hat. It was all the same thing.

Julio was just into second gear when I finally came sprinting up alongside the team bus, beating on its metal flank with my free hand and hissing through dry lips. After an eternity, someone finally noticed me. The big vehicle squealed to a stop and Julio threw the door wide open.

It was cold in the bus, damned cold after my recent dash through the hot streets. A veritable wall of chilled air coursed down the steps and enveloped me as I stood outside the bus door, catching my breath. Everyone was roaring with laughter, the whole damned team. There'd be another Cheetah Jones story going around the baseball world soon enough, another tale that'd grow taller with each telling. Which was fair enough, I supposed. My legend *should* grow, considering that my actual playing career was busily shrinking away to nothing.

My gorge was rising as I stood and panted, regaining my wind, and it took everything I had to climb the three steps up to where my team-mates sat. "Chee-*tah!*" my fellow players chanted. Clearly, they were aware that they were in the presence of genuine greatness, if of a rather bass-ackward kind. "Chee-*tah*! Chee-*tah*!" They high-handed me and grinned and laughed in delight as I lurched down the aisle, my face steadily turning green. Coach Melendez was sitting waiting for me in my usual seat, however. And he wasn't smiling at all.

It was just as well that I had the hat with me. Otherwise, I'd have barfed all over him.

Louisiana was every bit as damned hot as the Dominican Republic, I decided as I disembarked at the bustling Baton Rouge Metropolitan Airport. Even though it was still early spring a wall of heat greeted me as I clambered through the little suborbital's hatch. Almost immediately my back began itching again; it'd been doing so almost constantly for days now. The rocket I'd taken direct from Mexico City hadn't been important enough to rate a jetway; instead they'd simply rolled up a stairway-on-wheels and let us pick our luggage out of a pile as we passed by.

"Cheetah?" a familiar voice greeted me as I headed for the terminal, and for the first time since god knew when I smiled.

"Buster!" I declared, grinning like a kid at my former coach. Old Buster had been my mentor all the way from the single-A's on up. In fact, I'd kind of suspected that they'd moved him along with me just because we got along so well; once upon a time I'd been a top prospect and considered well-worth pampering. And he was with the Catfish now? They hadn't mentioned *that* in my call-up letter! "I thought you were still up in Ohio."

"Heck, no!" he declared, grinning. Then, ignoring my outstretched hand he threw his arms around me as if I were his long-lost son instead of a good prospect gone bad. I ignored the pain this caused the inflamed skin on my back; Buster was one of the few people in the world whom I'd allow to hug me. "The general manager up there was a real tightass. He even wanted everyone to cut their hair the same way." Buster shook his head, emphasizing the long, dark hair he still sported despite his age. "I finally got sick of it and decided to go someplace where they play real ball."

I snorted, pulling away from the embrace and beginning the long walk towards the terminal. "Come on, Buster. This is just a two-bit farm team like any other. We'll make a few bucks, have some good times and move on."

But Buster didn't move an inch. Suddenly, his face was very serious. "You got fired down in the Dominican, didn't you?" he asked. "For farting around?"

I shrugged. It hurt, but I didn't let it show. "Yeah. Well, I didn't do anything that everyone else wasn't."

"And before that, from the Mexican Leagues."

"They were pissants anyway."

"And before that, you only made it through half a season in Japan. Right?"

"My numbers were good there!" I objected. "The umps wanted to be treated like gods! Besides, I was leading the league in—"

"—geisha girls, rice wine and clubhouse turmoil," Buster continued smoothly. "But that wasn't your fault either, right?"

"You're damn right it wasn't! Anyone with any balls at all would've—"

"Would've, shmoud've," he interrupted me again. "Look, Cheetah. I've got good connections. No one else but me knows that you managed to get yourself canned down in the Dominican of all places. Besides, if you perform like I know you can out on the field then by the time anyone finds out they won't care anymore." He scowled, hard. "Damn it, Cheetah! You've got more natural talent than the good lord gave a whole team of Lou Brocks. I've never seen the like of you, when you quit making excuses and actually care about the game. Are you going to use your head this time around, or am I going to have to watch you flush away what is for absolute certain the last shot at glory you'll ever get?"

I looked down at the ground again, then smiled. "So, what's the deal?" I asked. "I mean, why did they call me up all of a sudden like this? And straight to triple-A, at that? I never figured to be back at all, much less up so high."

Buster sighed and looked away. "Your new owner is a certain Mr. James Sandrell," he explained. "Mr. Sandrell believes that the key to exciting, winning, stadium-filling baseball is speed. He hopes by next year or the year after to field a team full of base-stealers." Buster stared me in the eyes. "Someone dropped your name in his ear as one of the great unfulfilled prospects of the era. After all, you're still only twenty-seven. Though heaven knows that in your case it's not the years, it's the miles. So, he's giving you one last chance to show your stuff."

***

Cajun Field, located not far outside the heart of the bustling greater Baton Rouge metroplex, wasn't a bad place as minor-league fields went. The stadium was fairly old, and located downwind from a big gengineering outfit that spliced rice DNA with everything but the kitchen sink, producing franken-plants that grew alcohol, tailored lubricants, you name it. Pheew, did the place stink! But as Buster and I strolled up we could see workmen busily slapping on fresh paint, refurbishing the vending areas, and even repaving the parking lot.

"Mr. Sandrell is of the opinion that you get what you pay for," Buster explained as a bored-looking guard waved us through the front gate. "He believes that if he invests in his farm teams, they'll reward him with high-caliber, dedicated players."

I nodded absently, rubbernecking left and right as we headed down towards the training areas. The place was nearly empty save for the workmen; I'd been called into camp early. Finally, we walked past the entrance of the locker room to the corner where the coach had his little office.

". . .ain't gonna get no better than this!" he was shouting into a telephone when Buster swung the door open. My new boss was maybe sixty, though he looked half that age when he smiled. Save for a beer-belly, the barrel-chested old guy looked to be in pretty good shape. He smiled and waved at Buster, then spoke into the phone again. "You'll either deal or you won't deal. I don't care anymore. *Capish?*"

"But. . . But. . . But. . ." I heard a distant voice stammer.

"But nothing!" the coach replied. "Deal or don't—it's your decision." Then he slammed the device down onto his battered desk and stood up.

"Tony," Buster said, pressing me forward slightly. "This is Cheetah Jones. One of the most talented young men it's ever been my pleasure to coach." He turned to me. "Cheetah, meet Anthony Turnbull."

My eyes widened slightly as I reached forward to shake Turnbull's hand. He'd coached more than one major league team to a pennant; what he was doing down in the minors I hadn't a clue. Tony's grip was firm and his gaze steady.

"Cheetah," he greeted me with a nod. "Glad to have you, son. I've heard more remarkable things about you than you can imagine. Some of them are even about how you play the game." Then his face turned to stone. "What's this I hear about you getting fired down in the Dominican?"

I felt myself scowl. "It wasn't my fault," I explained. "There wasn't any alarm—"

"To hell with that!" Tony exploded. "You're a screw-up, Cheetah! You've never been anything *but* a screw-up, the whole time you've played ball. People I know and respect say you've got the makings in you. The genuine stuff, even." He nodded at Buster. "But you've got to get your head straight first. Or else you can walk out of here right now and never bother me again. Got me?"

My scowl deepened. I'd known up front that I'd have to put up with a lecture before they let me play again, but this was a lot worse than I'd expected.

"I'll take your sullen silence as a 'yes'," Tony continued after a moment had passed. His eyes narrowed. "Kid, do you have any idea of what kind of life you're throwing away? Of how many people there are in this country who'd gladly die for a chance at the majors?" He shook his head, then met my eyes again. "I've seen your kind come and go a dozen times over. Sometimes I don't know why I even bother trying anymore. But, every once in a great while, I find a player in the garbage pile worth the effort.

And then it all makes sense." There was another long silence before Tony spoke again. "You on the bottle, son? Drugs? Tell me the truth right now, and there'll be no consequences. We'll get you treatment, and so long as you work with us we'll work with you. I swear it! But if I find out later, I'll fire your butt in a heartbeat. I won't have a liar in my dugout. Not for all the stolen bases in the world."

"I drink," I replied evenly. "I drink hard, even. But not all that often. Maybe once a month, when I'm having a bad day. Other than that, it's just a beer or two now and then."

"Not anymore," Coach Turnbull replied. "As of right now you're on the wagon for the season. If I ever catch the faintest whiff of liquor on your breath, you can go file for unemployment in Santa Domingo for all I care."

"You can't—" I began.

"The hell you say!" Tony countered. "I can and will fire you for any reason I see fit, even if it's because the laundry screwed up my jockstrap and I feel a little itchy that day. Wait until you see your contract! It's loaded with more reasons for me to fire you than you can shake a stick at. There's even a moral terpitude clause!"

My lips tightened. "My agent—"

"—is grateful as hell to be getting *anything* out of a dead-loss client like you." Turnbull smiled. "Go ahead, Jones. Walk out." He crossed his arms. "I have other, better prospects that aren't pains in the butt. See if I care."

For a long moment we tried to stare each other down. Then I remembered who was holding all the aces and lowered my eyes. "All right," I agreed, phrasing things very carefully. "If you catch me drinking, I'm gone. Fair warning, and all that."

He nodded.

"But that moral terpitude thing. . ."

"Cripes!" Buster exploded. "Cheetah, the reason you went to Japan was because you got caught porking the owner's daughter on the shower floor! By the press, even! They got it on film! You've gotta be reasonable, here!"

I waved a patient hand. "It's not like that, Buster. Not like that at all." I turned back to Tony. "You said I could unload about booze and drugs right now, and not have it be held against me. Right?"

He nodded. "Yep."

I smiled uneasily and shrugged my shoulders. The skin on my back was beginning to itch again. Wouldn't the damned thing *ever* heal up? "Does that go for other things, too?"

He crossed his arms and looked interested. "Try me. I haven't heard a new one in ages. Though you might be just the guy to do it. I'll give you that much."

My smile widened. Despite myself, I was beginning to feel like this was a man I might be able to get along with. "You see, I picked up this tattoo one night in the Dominican Republic. The night before I got fired, in fact. I don't even remember getting the thing, and. . . Man! You won't *believe*. . ."

***

"I don't *believe* it!" the team doctor declared. I'd been hearing that exact phrase all afternoon, first from coaches, then from trainers, and now from the doc. "I simply do *not* believe it!"

"It's really there all right," I reassured him. "Trust me to be the one who would know for absolute certain."

Doctor Jorgenson shook his head. "I've heard of these things, but. . ."

I sighed. It *was* quite a tattoo, I had to admit, one that pushed the limits of the new electro-cellular tech. "It itches all the damn time," I complained.

"It probably always will," Doc Jorgensen replied, his voice sounding sad. "The idiot who applied the thing ran the power lines so close to a major nerve trunk that I'm surprised you're not in agony every time the ah, ah. . ."

"Every time the girl sorta lights up and rolls her eyes?" Buster asked.

"Which girl?" Doc Jorgensen countered, his lips wrinkled in distaste. Then he shook his head. "There isn't a thing I can do for you, Cheetah. That. . . That abomination is rooted way down inside you. To ablate it, I'd have to cut so deep that it'd be weeks, maybe even months, before you got your full range of motion back. If then. And your back would be half scar tissue when I was done."

"Jesus," Buster muttered. Then he turned to me. "For god's sake, kid? Why did you go and mess yourself up like that? Them things ain't even legal in the States!"

"And for good reason!" the doc agreed.

"It wasn't my fault," I explained. "I was drunk, see? I don't remember much about how it happened, except that the needle stung like the devil and that the artist's wife made one fine margarita."

"He can't hide it," Jorgensen pointed out needlessly. After all, Buster and Turnbull and I had figured it out long since. "Not in a locker room environment. The press'll be all over it in a week, maybe less." The doc frowned. "Frankly, I've never seen anything more ludicrously obscene in all my years. And I haven't exactly been a choir boy."

Buster frowned too, then crossed his arms in decision. "He can't play like that. It's simply not possible. What if the kids heard about it? Baseball is a family sport."

I nodded. So my trip up north was for nothing after all, it seemed. I'd finally gone and done it, screwed myself up so bad that no one in baseball would have me. I'd messed up in the majors, Japan, Mexico, the Dominican Republic and now here in Baton Rouge. And for what? A tattoo I couldn't even remember asking for?

". . .refund your airfare," Buster was saying, his face more deeply wrinkled than I ever remembered seeing it before. "And I can probably get you two weeks pay for showing up, seeing as how upper management still thinks you quit a good job to come."

"Right," I agreed. Two weeks pay? Well, I'd been fired before, hadn't I? Two weeks pay would buy me a nice bender and a hotel room for three, maybe four days to enjoy it. And then I could. . .

. . .do what? There wasn't anyplace left to run. Or at least not anyplace where I could play baseball.

Suddenly I felt a winter chill inside. "Look," I said, turning back to the doc. "I know you can't abrade this thing, or whatever the heck it was that you said. I understand that. But can't you do anything else? Like tattoo over it, say? Make it a great big black spot? Or else cover it up somehow?"

Doc Jorgenson pressed his lips together. "I'm sorry, Cheetah. You can't tattoo over one of these electro-cellular jobs. The thing will burn its way back through in days, if not hours. It's actually *alive*, you see. So long as it lives, it'll use every resource at its disposal to display the, ah, message it's programmed with. Since it's a form of parasite drawing on your body for energy, the more you mess with it the worse the drain on your body becomes. Trying to submerge it in black ink not only wouldn't work but would also make you sick as can be along the way. If the tattoo ever dies, which is very unlikely indeed, you have to ablate it immediately. With the unfortunate results we discussed earlier."

Jesus Christ! "What about covering it up? Look, maybe I could wear a bandage or something all the time, even in the shower."

"The area involved is far too large," Jorgensen explained. "Especially for a professional athlete. Your movements would be restricted. Eventually, a corner would come off." He frowned. "And with *that* thing, even just a corner would be quite enough."

"How about if we grew new skin over it?" I demanded, clutching at straws. One more bender, then the whole gaping future ahead, empty, empty, empty! "Like, over a burn? Don't they use nanites or some junk like that?"

"Yes," the team doctor agreed. "But we're still talking about a long period when you'd be unable to play. Just about the same amount of time that it'd take for the tattoo to burn back through, most likely. About the only thing. . ." Suddenly, Jorgenson's voice trailed off, his eyes narrowed, and he raised his right hand to his chin. "Maybe. Just maybe. . ."

"What?" I asked, suddenly desperate. Good god, what was I going to do with myself? Become a truck driver? A hamburger flipper? Deal drugs on the streets back home and have kids point at me and talk about who I used to be? How could I *live*, without baseball? "I'll try anything! Anything at all, even if it might kill me!"

"This wouldn't kill you," the doctor replied. "Not exactly." Then he sighed. "All right, Cheetah. I've got an idea. But I have to do a little research before I can say anything more. And you're going to have to be pretty open-minded for it to work." He turned to Buster. "So is the team, for that matter."

"I still can't believe I'm doing this," Coach Turnbull declared as our insanely aggressive autotaxi darted left and right through the heavy New York City traffic. I'd never ridden in an autotaxi before; we'd left my stomach behind several swerves back. Judging by his pallor, Tony had the same problem.

"*You* can't believe *you're* doing this?" I countered angrily. "I'm the one that's going to have to put up with all the catty remarks and teasing and stuff. . ." I sighed, then for about the tenth time made a conscious effort relax back into my seat. But it was impossible; every time I tried my tattoo stung like a wasp.

"You think all of it's going to be on you?" Tony countered. "The other coaches are going to give me more lip than you—"

"Now approaching Freedom Center," the pleasant and incongruously female voice of the autotaxi interrupted as it swerved hard right, squealing its tires and setting off a veritable symphony of horn-blowing. "Please have your fare in hand and be ready to depart the vehicle promptly. Thank you for choosing the Yellow Checkers Cab Company."

"Right," Tony muttered, digging out his credit card. Neither of us had any luggage, this being a mere day-trip. "I still don't believe it. Here I've got my whole lineup checking into training camp today, and where am I? Sitting in a cab in New York alongside the biggest screw-up in baseball getting ready to beg permission to—"

The cab lurched hard left, once again igniting a wave of protests. "Five," the sweet, gentle voice intoned. "Four. Three. Two. One. . ."

. . .and the automated vehicle came screeching to a halt right in the middle of a traffic lane! More horns blared as Tony clumsily ran his card through the reader; he had to do it twice because he got rattled and dropped it the first time. Then we went dashing for the curb, the little capsule nearly clipping me on the ankle as it blasted away under full acceleration.

"Jesus!" Tony muttered once we were safely ensconced on the sidewalk. His head swiveled left, then right again; clearly, he was more than a little out of his depth. Finally, he nodded firmly towards a large entryway off to the left. "That way," he declared.

"Right," I agreed, leading off. Between suborbital flights, autocabs and waiting around at airports I'd been in Tony's close company for almost six hours already and had at least another six to go. It wasn't much fun at all, and if I could put him out of my sight by walking a little faster then he did, so much the better. I was maybe halfway to the big public entrance when I heard a squeaky voice cry out. "Cheetah!" it declared. "Cheetah Jones! Wait up!"

I practically froze in my tracks; who did I know in New York, anyway? Then Tony stopped close up behind me, and I amended the question. Who did I know in New York that was about to embarrass me to the quick in front of my new coach? A hooker? Someone I owed money to? A former drinking buddy, now begging on the street?

But it turned out that the voice belonged to none of the above; instead, it was the property of a pimply-faced boy of about fourteen. "Cheetah!" he declared again as he came rolling up in his power-chair, middle-aged mother bustling up behind him. "I knew it was you just as soon as I saw you get out of that cab. I knew it!" He grinned from ear to ear.

I cocked my head to one side. "You know me?" I asked.

"Sure!" he declared. "You played with the Springfield Minutemen for what, five months?" He looked back at his mother. "I've got your card in my collection. Too bad it's at home."

"He'd bring his cards everywhere, if I let him," the kid's mother explained. She looked down at his shriveled legs. There were darned few crippled people left in the world who couldn't be helped with modern tech, but this young man was clearly one of them. "They mean the world to him."

My head nodded slowly. I hated being around crippled people. They weirded me out. "I see."

"You were the fastest player in the majors!" the kid exulted. "Still probably would be, if you hadn't gone for the money in Japan." His face fell a little. "Do you like it over there?"

Just then my companion cleared his throat, and I introduced him. "This is Tony Turnbull," I explained. "Coach of—"

"The world champion San Jose Toros!" the kid cried out in exultation, his eyes bugging in pleasure. "Oh, wow! What a great day this is! I'm so sorry I didn't recognize you, Mr. Turnbull! I've got your card too, of course. But once I saw Cheetah. . ."

Tony handled the situation with all the class I didn't have. "Sure thing, kid," he said with a smile, leaning over and extending a hand for his young fan to shake. "What's your name?"

"Raymond!" he exclaimed. "Raymond Belanger! I'm from New Hampshire; we're just down here to see a specialist."

"Right," Tony continued, his smile never cracking for an instant. "Do you by any chance ever get down to Boston?"

"Sometimes," he answered, looking a little puzzled.

"Well," Tony continued. "I have a colleague there who can make special arrangements. And, it so happens, she owes me a favor." He pulled out a little piece of paper and scrawled rapidly on it. "If you were to call my friend Angela at this number in a few days, after I've had time to make a call or two of my own," he explained, "you might just get to watch a major league game from the dugout."

Young Raymond's eyes widened until I thought they were about to pop out of his head. *"Wow!"*

Then he scribbled a little more. "And," he continued, "if you were to send Cheetah's and my baseball cards to this address here, there's a distinct possibility that they might come back autographed, too. With pictures, even." He paused thoughtfully and looked at me. "Though you might want to wait a few months on his," he added. "Or maybe not. Who knows? Maybe it'll be more valuable *this* way."

"I. . . Uh. . ." Raymond was totally at a loss for words, it seemed. But his mother wasn't.

"Thank you!" she gushed. "Oh, thank you so very much!"

"No problem," Tony replied, doffing his cap and smiling one last time. Then he made a great show of looking at his watch. "I'm sorry, folks. But. . ."

"Oh!" Mrs. Belanger gushed. "Don't let us hold you up! And thank you again, one last time. Thank you *so* much!"

"No problem," Turnbull assured her. "Our privilege." And then we were walking side-by-side towards the door.

"Jeez!" I said once we were out of earshot. "You pretty much shot the wad for that kid."

He shrugged. "It's what's expected."

I pressed my lips together. "Maybe it's what's expected of *you*," I answered evenly. "But you're not getting paid league minimum. Coach, I get twenty bucks for an autograph! And here you promised that Raymond kid one for free!"

Turnbull stopped dead in his tracks. Then, very slowly he turned around. "Cheetah," he said quietly. "I have met some real world-class jerks in my life. But you, you miserable jackass, have just taken the cake."

"Why?" I demanded. "Lots of players charge for autographs!"

"Are you *blind*?" he demanded at the top of his lungs, totally ignoring the stares of the pedestrians detouring around us. "On top of every other screwed-up thing about you? Am I going to have to send a seeing-eye dog out into the field with you, to lead you to the balls?"

"So he was in a wheelchair!" I countered angrily, my own voice rising. Damnit, I was *entitled* to autograph money, when and if I could ever make any! "Big deal!"

Turnbull's eyes narrowed, then he looked down at the sidewalk. "Jesus," he whispered. "You really *didn't* see." Then he looked up again; this time there was a tear running down his cheek. "The kid was wearing a Cancer Society medallion around his neck," he explained. "And his mom was carrying a bunch of pamphlets. Pamphlets about hospice programs for children. Do you know what a hospice program is, or are you stupid, too? Do you need me to connect the dots?"

My mouth fell open, then closed again. "He's going to die?" I asked.

"Yes, he *is* going to die," Tony replied, looking dead into my eyes. "And if you'd paid half as much attention to that poor kid as he so clearly did to you, if you'd cared half as much about what is probably the one single solitary fan you have left in this world as he did about you and your pitiful excuse for a career, you'd have figured that out all by your lonesome."

I blinked. "That kid is going to *die*?"

"Jesus!" Tony declared, rolling his eyes in frustration. Then he pulled out his wallet, removed a twenty, and slapped it into my hand. "Payment for the autograph," he explained. "In advance." Then he turned and stomped away.

And no matter how hard I tried, he wouldn't take the money back.

***

James Sandrell, my team's owner, was clearly a very busy and important man. His offices were up near the top of the Freedom Center. Once we got past the public areas, the place looked as if a mahogany-eating dragon had vomited all over the inside. I'd never even *heard* of such expensive furnishings.

Even Tony seemed a little overawed as we made our way back to the innermost sanctum of TransGenics Incorporated's office suite. He shuffled his feet and spoke nervously, in short little sentences. "Be quiet unless spoken to, Cheetah! Don't screw this up. It's all in the bag, if you'll just keep your trap shut. And try not to damage anything!"

At least Mr. Sandrell didn't keep us waiting; the secretary ushered us right in. "He's on a conference call to Europe," he explained, smiling politely. "But Mr. Sandrell hates to be kept waiting in anterooms and therefore tries to avoid causing others the same discomfort."

Tony nodded and thanked the secretary, stuttering abominably. Then the heavy door swung open, and we were inside. "Hi!" Mr. Sandrell greeted us from behind what looked to me like quite an ordinary, unexceptional desk. His voice was deep and rich. "I'll be right with you guys!"

"Sure," my coach agreed, smiling. "Take your time."

Sandrell grinned back, then returned his attention to the transatlantic call. He was a much younger man than I'd expected, maybe forty, with a coffee-colored complexion and perfect white teeth that flashed attractively when he smiled. "I say it's a go on the new mutagenic sequence," he said into the telephone. "We've passed every test that the EU can possibly throw at us. Our product is safe and effective." There was a long pause as someone on the other end of the line said his or her piece, then Sandrell spoke again. "Yes, of course. That's a given. But how much will it cost us *not* to move up production, assuming the pro-cess *is* approved? Which I firmly believe that it will be. There's risk in everything, Maria. And there are consequences both to acting and to not-acting. I've always preferred the former." There was another short pause, then he smiled. "Fine, Maria, fine indeed! Then that is how we shall do it. Forgive me, but I have important business waiting in the office here." His face lit up. "Baseball business! My very favorite kind! Thank you, and good-bye. Hasta la vista!" And with that, he returned the instrument to its charger. "Forgive me, gentlemen," he explained. "I know that we had an appointment. But business can sometimes be pressing."

"Of course," Tony answered for us both. "Believe me, both of us regret having to take up *any* of your valuable time on minor-league stuff."

"Nonsense!" the executive countered, gesturing for us to sit down. "Baseball is my passion, even at the minor league level. Besides, today's minor-leaguer is tomorrow's star." He turned to me and extended a hand. "Cheetah, it is a true pleasure to meet you at long last. I saw you play in Springfield, several times."

I've never known what to say when someone tells me that, so I just nodded, shook the offered hand, and smiled. I couldn't help but be aware of Tony watching me like a hawk. Somehow, I knew that at the slightest misstep he stood ready to interrupt.

"Your style of play was incredibly aggressive," Sandrell continued. "Angry, even. In the course of the three games I was able to attend, you stole seven bases and were thrown out once. At home plate," he added quietly.

My mouth instantly jumped into gear. I'd only once tried to steal home in the majors, so I knew exactly the incident he was referring to. "It wasn't my fault!" I explained. "And I was safe, too." Then Tony's heel ground into the top of my foot and I shut up again.

"I think that you were safe, as well," the team's owner replied, a twinkle in his eye. "And I had a better angle on the play than the ump did." He shrugged. "But that's all water under the bridge, is it not? Umps make bad decisions sometimes; after all, they're only human. Just as all of us are human. Putting bad decisions behind us, learning from them, and then moving on into the future is one of the key skills of life. Until it's mastered, little else is possible." He looked deep into my eyes but, mindful of Tony's heel I said nothing.

Then Sandrell sighed and leaned back into his chair. "Perhaps some explanations are in order, Cheetah. Many years ago I was a prospect myself. I was even signed onto a single-A team. I played the game much as you play it, wide open and with everything hanging out. I even sometimes sharpened my spikes." He smiled wistfully. "And then, before I ever played my first pro game, I did something stupid. Some of my friends asked me to go for a ride with them. I didn't know that the car was stolen. Nor did I know that some of the others were carrying guns. By the time I was clear of the law the season was well underway and the team had, quite understandably, lost interest in me."

Tony nodded. "I'm very sorry, sir." He glanced around the expensive office. "But things seem to have come out all right for you in the end."

"Heh!" the billionaire snorted. "One might say so. And then again one might not." He opened a desk drawer and pulled out a dusty old fielder's glove. "I still play ball, you know. In an executive's league. Center field. For the sheer love of the game."

"Good for you, sir," Tony said.

"Yes," Sandrell agreed. "Good. But not as good as it might've been." He gestured all around him. "I love this corporation. Even more, I love what it can do for people and what this new technology means to the future of mankind." Then he turned to face me. "But never doubt for a second that I'd gladly trade it all for the chance to try and steal home plate with the game on the line against Sasquatch Howard pitching and Tom Bowan catching, blind umpire be damned."

He was staring right at me, but somehow I had nothing to say. Finally Tony stomped down on my foot, hard. "I see," I said slowly.

"Maybe," Sandrell replied. "Maybe you do see, and maybe you don't. But I propose to find out." His mouth formed a thin, hard line. "Cheetah, once upon a time you impressed me to no end. And, perhaps I see a bit of myself in you. Just in case there's any doubt at all remaining in your mind, let me make it clear to you that you are where you're at today because I've pulled a thousand strings on your behalf. Is that understood?"

I gulped and nodded. So, having Buster pick me up at the airport *hadn't* been a coincidence? "Yes, sir."

"Now don't go getting any ideas that this means I'll tolerate any nonsense from you." He turned to Tony. "As much as you mean to me, your coach means far more. I've instructed him to give you one, and only one, more chance. I'll interfere to no greater extent than that, and if he chooses to let you go then I'll not only back him to hilt, but I'll also apologize for having stepped on his toes in the first place. There's no one in baseball I respect more than him." Then he sighed. "But so much for the best-laid plans of mice and men." He shook his head. "What on earth *ever* possessed you to get that incredible tattoo?"

I looked down at my shoes. "I don't even remember. It may have been the stupidest thing I've ever done."

Sandrell nodded. "Good. You're being honest. *That* we can work with." He turned to Tony. "You say that you have a plan for dealing with this issue?"

Tony nodded. "Yes, sir. We plan to cover the tattoo, very effectively and thoroughly, so that no one will ever know. With fur." He smiled hopefully. "We even plan on using products from your company. So, you could maybe. . . Sorta sponsor it."

Sandrell's eyes widened for a moment, then he grinned wide and leaned back in his chair. "It could be done, of course. The technology is totally proven. We do up actors for movies all of the time. And then there are the exotic dancers. . ." He turned to me. "You'd be willing to go through with this?"

I nodded.

"It's against league rules to modify the human body in such a way as to improve athletic performance," the executive mulled. "If we were careful, we could leave your basic structure untouched. In fact, if we played it smart we'd make you just a tiny bit weaker, so that no one could complain on those grounds."

"Our team doctor has put together a package," Tony explained. "Cheetah here would miss about three weeks of the pre-season in hospital. By the time he got out, he'd have enough fur to cover the tattoo. Though of course he won't completely finish changing until September or so."

"Right," Sandrell mused, his eyes distant. Then he grinned. "You know, this has real possibilities, far and away exceeding the mere covering up of a tattoo. The fans might just decide they love it. If we can get the league to go along with us, that is."

"And if Cheetah can play effectively as, well, a cheetah," Tony pointed out. "After all, even as a normal human. . ."

"Right," Sandrell agreed again. Then he came to a decision. "Begin the treatment," he directed. "Cosmetic body modifications have never been against league rules and when you get right down to it this is purely cosmetic, even if a little on the extreme side. I'll do a little back-door politicking, and then we'll present the other owners with a *fait accompli*." He looked at me again. "Expect stormy weather, son. I think you're going to find that there's a lot more involved in making big changes in one's self than you yet realize."

"There's a lot more involved in making big changes in one's self than you yet realize," the doctor explained to me as I lay waiting in bed. I smiled, having heard that one before. "For one thing, you simply *must* get used to being looked at naked. By me, especially. That'll be happening more and more as we go on."

I blushed; Dr. Henway was a pretty young lady, and they not only had me in a hospital gown but one that was too short by several inches. Or at least I thought so. Plus, they'd already made a pincushion out of me. I'd never even imagined getting so many injections so fast! "I'm sorry," I answered, very slowly easing the sheet back. "You see, I was still in New York just this morning, and—"

"—and they're pushing you just as hard as they're pushing me," she replied evenly. "Rush, rush, rush! After all, I woke up in Spokane myself, with my husband. And, I can assure you, the last place I thought I'd finish out my day was in Baton Rouge, Louisiana." Then the doctor smiled. "Well, my recruiter *told* me that working for TransGenics would be interesting and exciting." Her face grew serious again. "Stand up, turn around, and open up your gown. I want to see this famous tattoo of yours."

I gritted my teeth, then did as ordered. It was freezing in my hospital suite, absolutely freezing. The soles of my feet stuck to the linoleum as I solemnly swiveled, gritted my teeth, and opened the fllmsy garment.

"Oh. . . My. . . God!" my doctor whispered in awe. Suddenly she sounded about sixteen. "That is *so* incredible!"

"It itches all of the time," I pointed out. "Even aches. I don't suppose that you can—"

"Sure," she replied. "I'll add an extra sheathing to the affected nerve; they've already told me it gives you trouble. And the fur-job will cover it up just fine. Don't worry about *that*. I plan to make yours extra–thick, just to make sure." Then she paused for a long moment as I stood and shivered. "Your build and musculature are perfect for a cheetah," she went on after a time.

"Long arms and legs, very thin torso, even your head won't have to be reshaped too much. Except for the muzzle, of course."

"Muzzle?" I countered. "Look, lady! I agreed to a coat of fur, yes. But—"

"And the tail ought to be fine as well. You don't have even a trace of scoliosis." I heard her scribbling on something. "If I didn't know better, I'd say that you were a professional athlete in the prime of life." There was a long pause, during which I said nothing. "That was a joke, Mr. Jones. Sorry. You can get back into bed, if you like."

I took her up on it in a flash, noticing that Dr. Henway's eyes followed me intently the whole time. "Do you have any films of yourself running?" she asked. "I mean, out on the field?"

"There might be some in the archives," I replied. "Why?" Then my eyes narrowed. "What kind of doctor are you, anyway?"

"I'm your body sculptor," she replied, smiling prettily. "It'll be my job to design the new you. Detail work, like locating your spots and such. Mostly I do exotic dancers. No one's ever done a pro athlete before. I can't believe that Mr. Sandrell asked for me personally on your case. It's such an honor!" She smiled again. "You can call me Kris, if you'd like."

I nodded. "All right, Kris. But listen to me. No muzzle. No tail. I agreed to the fur, yes. But no more than that. Got it?"

Dr. Henway's face fell. "Didn't you know?" Her eyes darted back and forth. "Mr. Jones. . . You've already received the basic injections. Mr. Sandrell gave the go-ahead and I know for fact that you signed the papers. I verified them myself before we gave you the shot; professional ethics and all that, you know."

I closed my eyes and sighed, remembering the endless stream of legal-looking documents that Coach Turnbull had passed across to me for signing on the flight home. I'd stopped to read one of them; it had relieved everyone in the entire universe, including yet-undiscovered alien intelligences, of legal liability for potential brain damage. "It's not like anyone would know the difference anyway!" Tony'd snapped. "Sign the thing, or else go try and find a new league to play in. It's up to you, Jones. Frankly, I don't care anymore. I've got better things to do."

So, I'd resumed signing without reading. Until it was done.

"I'm a body *sculptor*, not a body *designer*," Kris explained. "All I do is tweak the details, to make the transition safe and artistically pleasing. It takes a whole team and lots of computer time to set up a whole new design. If we hadn't just happened to have the basic cheetah-form on file already, we wouldn't have been able to get any of this done. You see, there's this gay dance club in San Fransisco where. . ." Her words trailed off, and she blinked twice. "Anyway, Mr. Jones, the new basic layout is already in your bloodstream and it can't be reversed. Everyone here seems to think that this was done with your permission." She paused. "Don't tell me that in this insane rush, no one. . ."

I sighed and looked down. "I probably *did* sign the papers," I admitted. "I just didn't bother to read them first. So, don't worry; you've done nothing wrong." Then I met her eyes. "Not that it probably would've made any difference if I'd memorized them. They've really got my ass in a crack. Or else I've got my own ass in a crack; the truth is, I'm not even really sure which anymore." I thought about young Raymond in his wheelchair for some odd reason, and then my vision blurred. Perhaps it was the drugs. In any case, once I wiped my eyes I could see all right again. "But whichever, it looks like I'm going to be changing a lot more than I ever planned for."

Dr. Henway nodded, pretending that she understood what I meant. "There's a whole package of treatments associated with this procedure," she explained. "Physical therapy, mandatory counseling. . . The program is very supportive." She smiled again. "I think you'll be fine, Mr. Jones. You seem much more stable than several other transformees I've sculpted."

I nodded and smiled back at her despite my apprehensions. Mandatory counseling! Just what I friggin' needed right in the middle of attempting a comeback. What a waste of time! But it was that or the highway, it seemed. I'd already been warned that if I was in any way uncooperative with the medical people, there were a dozen other prospects salivating for my spot in the lineup.

"So," I continued, "I'm getting a muzzle and tail to go with the fur." The words felt odd coming out of my mouth. But still, there were worse things in the universe, I supposed. Like going back to the Dominican and begging for my old job back. *Or being a suffering kid in a wheelchair that was never, ever going to grow up,* a little voice whispered in my ear. "I can live with that, I guess. Anything a gay exotic dancer can take, I can take." I smiled reassuringly at Kris, who seemed a little relieved. "But please, tell me right now. How far is this going to go on the rest of me?" I suddenly felt very aware of my body as it shifted slightly against the clean soft sheets. Up until then, somehow, the whole change-thing hadn't felt real. But. . . *The drugs were already in my veins,* she'd told me. *Already in my veins. . .*

How exactly would lying in this same bed feel, I wondered, with a layer of soft fur between my skin and the sheets? Not bad at all, I was suddenly certain.

Maybe this whole cheetah-thing might have some interesting aspects, after all.

***

They promised me I'd only be in the hospital for three weeks. By noon on the second day I started to go itchy all over, not just on top of my tattoo, and by two in the afternoon I was out for the count, not to be brought back around for seventeen days. They kept me in a full life-support tank all of that time, while every cell in my body was reprogrammed and, in some cases, taught a whole new way of life. Not that I noticed; all I ever remembered of it was having the same dream over and over again. In it I stood in front of my fourth grade teacher with a Mexican-style sombrero in my hands, barfing my guts out while she glared at me with Buster's eyes and the rest of the class chanted "Chee-*tah*! Chee-*tah*! Chee-*tah*!" At least I got paid for those three weeks, full rate. And for those same twenty-one days Coach Turnbull found no fault with me. Somehow, I figured that would end up being the all-time record.

When they finally woke me up, my tattoo was covered with cheetah-patterned fur all right, just as thick and full as promised. So was my chest, for that matter. And my back, and my legs, and my face, and my arms. . .

"Hey!" I protested to Dr. Henway as she bustled by on my first afternoon of wakefulness. "Wait up a second."

"Sure, Mr. Jones," she replied smoothly, not sounding at all frustrated despite the fact that I'd stopped her in exactly the same way six other times in the past hour. "What can I do for you?"

"These hands!" I complained, holding up the offending body parts and wriggling them vigorously, just like I'd already done with several other bits of my anatomy. "There's fur all over the palm side! How in the world can I be expected grab a baseball and throw it like this? I can't even get a decent grip on my water glass, for Christ's sake!"

"You'll have to shave them every morning," Kris replied pertly. "Instead of your face. We'll show you how to do it before you leave our care. But that's only temporary, of course. You'll have the beginnings of your paw-pads growing in a couple weeks. They'll be a little sore and tender at times, but at least you can quit shaving your hands then. The pads won't grow fur."

"Paw. . . Paw. . . Paw. . ." I stuttered, but just like the other six times, Dr. Henway was gone before I could formulate the rest of my question. You'd have thought she considered me an unpleasant person to be around or something!

But that wasn't the worst. I had to spend a whole afternoon with Dr. Forster before they'd let me leave. He was a shrink.

"So," he said with a smile, leaning easily up against his desk. "Your nickname has always been Cheetah, eh? It's not just a baseball thing?"

"Kind of," I agreed after a long moment of silence.

"Kind of?" the therapist countered. "How so?"

I frowned. Since whiskers were also hair cells I'd already grown them along with the fur. The stupid things tingled and itched whenever I moved my mouth. It was even more annoying than the tattoo had been, though everyone assured me I'd get used to them in no time flat. "Well. . ."

The silence stretched out again, until Dr. Forster spoke again. "Did they call you that because you've always been fast?"

"No." Another long pause. This time it dragged on and on and on, until I began to wonder if the damned doc was trying to bore me to death. "At first, they called me 'Cheater'," I finally explained. "Everyone did. But once I moved away from home, I managed to get people to change it to 'Cheetah'. You don't want people calling you 'Cheater' when you play ball for a living. It gives people the wrong idea."

"Ah," Dr. Forster answered, a big fake smile painted onto his kisser. "I can see where that might be a problem."

There was another long silence, and I stirred awkwardly in my seat. Geez! What a bore this guy was! And I was going to have to keep seeing him all season long, twice a week? Maybe being unemployed in the Dominican Republic wasn't so bad after all! "My brother started it," I finally explained, just to fill the empty silence. "When I broke one of his toys. It was a little car that his grandma gave him. Then I fixed things up so that Mom would think he did it, so that it wouldn't be my fault. All of the kids on our street found out, and soon everyone was calling me that."

"Did the other kids like you?" my therapist asked.

"No," I answered, half-smiling. "I was always the fastest and the strongest, see? I won all the races, even with kids a year or two older than me. Since I was so strong, they couldn't outrun or outfight me either one. So mostly they were afraid of me."

"You must've been a very angry young man," Dr. Forster observed.

I shrugged and half-chuckled. "Maybe," I allowed. "Not that it did me any good. Mom was always shacking up with these losers, see? Pathetic no-goods, every one. Most of them druggies; none had jobs. With them it didn't matter how fast and strong I was. . ."

And so on and so forth. It was the biggest waste of time imaginable; if only the team paid *me* half as much an hour as it was paying my shrink! When Dr. Henway interrupted us because it was time to show me how to shave my hands, I was never so glad to see anyone in my life! At least all she wanted was to show me how to live with the cheetah-stuff I had to do, instead of asking questions about my true name and who I really was, deep down inside.

5

When the hospital finally released me, they sent a note to Coach Turnbull. He wasn't very happy when he opened it. "Light duty?" he asked, looking me directly in the eyes. Then he turned away; my peepers were deep gold now. They were the only part of the whole cheetah-thing I really liked so far. "What is this, Cheetah? You're already behind everyone else."

I shrugged. "It don't mean nothing to me, Coach," I replied. "I'll do whatever you want. The fact is, I didn't even open the envelope."

"Hrmm," Tony mumbled, pressing his lips together. Then he pushed a button on his desk. "Herman!" he demanded. "You busy?"

"Not at the moment," a youthful voice replied from the intercom box. "What can I do for you?"

"Cheetah's back from the hospital. He's got some kind of note from his doc. I need a trainer's opinion of what he can do and what he can't. We're in my office."

"Cool!" Herman exclaimed. "I can't wait to see him!"

I hadn't met Herman yet, but when he came bustling down the hall there was no doubt in my mind whatsoever as to who he was. Look up "nerd athlete wannabe" in the dictionary; the last time I checked his picture was still there. "Wow!" he declared once he stepped through the door, looking me up and down over and over again. "That came out *well*!"

"Thanks," I mumbled. Just about everyone seemed to think I looked good in spots, even though all I had so far was the fur. My ears hadn't begun to migrate yet, nor did I have even the nub of a tail.

"Look!" Tony exclaimed, slamming the note down for Herman to read. "No running. No heavy exercise. No *emotional stress*, for chrissakes! What am I supposed to do with this? I run a baseball team, not a girl's school!" He gestured at me. "Cheetah here seems cooperative enough," he added, just to be fair. "I don't think it's his fault. Maybe we can just ignore most of this crap?"

Herman smiled. My new trainer was much older than his voice and mannerisms would indicate, and the expression did nice things to the wrinkles in his face. "We'll work something out," he promised. Then he looked me over more carefully. I was wearing shorts and an armless shirt, all that was comfortable between the hot weather and the fur. In a few days, I was told, jillions of little nano-heat-exchangers would kick in to help keep my body temp where it belonged, and I'd quit perspiring entirely. For the moment, though, I simply dressed for high summer even though it was still spring. "You've got excellent muscle definition, Cheetah," he proclaimed. "The fur seems to enhance it more than anything else."

I shrugged. "Whatever."

"Not much fat on you, either," he continued. "They do a pretty good job these days, maintaining conditioning while you're in a life support tank. And, you were playing pro ball just a few weeks back, weren't you? Fully in training?" he asked.

I nodded. "Yep."

"Good," Herman agreed. He turned to Tony. "We'll work something out," he promised again. "If I'm any judge, physically he's ready to play right now. Most likely it's just some little hitch with the transformation process. And the team's bought into that, right? So, I've just gotta call the doc first and see what's going on. Plus, I really oughta sit down and have a heart-to-heart with Buster about where to take Cheetah's regimen. Give me until tomorrow to come up with a personal training plan. Okay?"

"Humph!" Tony snorted. Then he frowned and nodded. "All right," he agreed. "Cheetah goes to work tomorrow. But today he can hang around the field at least." Then the coach looked at me. "I've cut a deal with the press, on the side, like. They're gonna leave you alone for now, as a favor to me personally. So that's at least something you won't have to deal with right away. Though god knows they're gonna be all over that spot-job of yours sooner or later." Then Tony turned back to Herman. "He can get to know the rest of the team and draw his uniform and gear. Can you walk him through that?”

“Sure!” the trainer agreed, smiling like a kid. He seemed like the happiest guy in the world, Herman did, despite the fact that probably wasn't getting paid squat to be a trainer on a minor-league team. “Come on, Cheetah! I'll show you your locker and everything!”

***

Two hours later I was just finishing putting on my spanking-new jersey. The thing fit as if it’d been custom tailored, despite the fact that I'd never been measured. I wondered how it was they'd managed that, until Herman proudly explained that it’d been his idea to call the hospital and have them measure me while I was still in the tank. He'd chattered my ears off, Herman had, nattering on endlessly about this and that like an old woman until eventually duty had taken him away. “You're going to love being with the Catfish,” the young-old man predicted, slapping me on the back. “We're more a family than a ball team. Mr. Sandrell buys us the best of everything—you ought to see my training room! And Coach Turnbull is a real professional, much better than anyone we've had before. But I'll let you change clothes now. I'm sure you can find your own way around a clubhouse.” And with that he was gone.

My locker was located just outside Coach Turnbull's window, where he could keep a close eye on me. Which was understandable enough, I supposed, even though it wasn't exactly what I might’ve chosen for myself. His and my eyes met several times while he stomped around hollering into his phone and I slowly changed clothes, still learning how to keep the fur lying straight wherever the fabric was snug. I was just looking down at the ridiculous anthropomorphic catfish emblazoned across my chest for the very first time ever when someone knocked on Turnbull's door. He was a big guy, I noted, and despite the suit and tie his youth and overall healthy glow marked him as a fellow athlete. Probably a catcher, I judged from his build, or else maybe a first baseman. And a power-hitter, to boot.

"Yeah?" Tony replied, not even turning around. "Come in."

"Hello," the new guy said shyly, stepping inside and not quite closing the door after him. I could hear every word. "I'm Pudge Hiller."

"Hiller!" Tony replied, smiling wide and slamming the phone down, cutting off cold whoever was on the other end. He extended his right arm, and my new teammate shook it. "I'm damned glad to see you, son! I traded half a team's worth of perfectly good prospects for you, and don't regret it a bit."

The big man blushed slightly. "I just want to play," he replied. "That's the truth."

"And play you will!" Tony replied, wrapping his right arm around Hiller and sitting down next to him. They had old home week for a little while as I put on my new cleats for the first time and adjusted them this way and that. I was a runner, after all. My cleats legitimately needed to be set up just right. I wasn't eavesdropping, oh no!

Why didn't Tony ever smile when he saw *me*?

". . .only one problem," the coach was explaining as I finally finished with my left foot and switched over to lacing up the right. "We already have a 'Pudge' on this team, son. Pudge Jefferson. You may have heard of him. He's a catcher too."

"I have," Hiller agreed. "He's a great man. I hope to learn a lot from him."

"That's why he's here," my coach explained. "His major league career may be over, but Pudge caught in the bigs for almost twenty-five seasons. He's more of a coach than a player these days, you see. Especially for the pitching staff. The man has four gold gloves to his credit, and while he and I both think it's a long shot Pudge just might end up taking a trip to Cooperstown someday." Then Tony sighed. "Hiller, I can't ask a man like that to change his nickname. I simply can't. Yet having two Pudge's on one team would be ridiculous, especially with both of them being catchers. Surely you can understand the position I'm in."

Hiller nodded. "I do."

Tony brightened. "Good! So, I checked your records, and everything says 'Pudge'. What's your real first name, anyway?"

Hiller blushed. "I was named after my mother's father. He was a great man, a doctor and philanthropist. There's a statue of him on our local town square. It was such an obvious thing at the time, me being named after him, that no one really thought—"

"I'm sure," Tony interrupted, still smiling. "What's your real name, son?"

"Adolph. My full legal name is Adolph Hiller."

You had to give Tony credit; his smile never wavered, even though he did blink. "*Adolph* Hiller? Your real, honest-to-god legal name is Adolph Hiller?"

"Uh-huh," the young giant replied, looking as if he were about to cry.

"Well. . ." Tony answered, frowning and looking down at the floor. Then his face brightened once more. "Welcome aboard, Pudge!" he declared, standing up and escorting his new catcher to the door. "Glad to have you aboard! I'll call Herman, our trainer; he'll have you all sorted out in no time. Batting practice is at three. See you there!"

***

The inside of a dugout is relatively dark compared to a sunny ball field. This makes it difficult for anyone out practicing to notice someone inside, especially if the person in question sits in the back row and remains relatively immobile. I'd taken full advantage of this fact many times in my baseball career, starting back in high school when I'd sat and rolled joints when I should've been shagging flies. So, despite the new fur it felt quite natural for me to slink along the dugout's back wall and then sit hunched-down on the end of the bench. Practically the whole team was working out; some were swinging bats under the watchful eyes of coaches, a little machine was pumping simulated fly balls into the outfield, and a remarkably young right-handed pitcher, eighteen years old if that, was standing out on the mound with his toe on the rubber, trying to hold a runner on first.

"Come on!" I heard the pitching coach cry out. "Smooth and sudden, like I know you can."

"Easy, son," Buster's voice countered from the first-base coaching box. "You can take a bigger lead than that. Be confident, be bold."

Despite myself, I sat up and paid closer attention. The runner at first was built just like me, I realized, sinewy and long of bone. But he wasn't leading off worth a damn. Then, when he finally decided to stretch things out he leaned so obviously that a nine-year-old could've picked him off.

Which was precisely what the kid on the mound did, smooth and sudden just as he'd been coached. His form blurred into motion, the brand-new ball made a long white streak in the air and there was a cloud of dust at first base. "Jeez!" Buster muttered; his runner had been thrown out by a foot or more.

The pitcher grinned, then turned to his beaming coach. "Good job, kid," the older man muttered.

Then they set up and did it again, and again, and again. Mostly the same thing happened. With each failure the runner became more hesitant, and his lead-off shrank to almost nothing. "Damnit!" Buster muttered to himself while the pitching coach called a time-out to work with his prospect on the finer points of things. Then he pursed his lips angrily.

I pursed my lips, too. Mr. Sandrell wanted to put a team together based on speed, I knew. The kid looked fast enough. But. . .

Finally I stood up and strolled leisurely out into the sun. Almost immediately I began sweating heavily under the fur. But how could I let Buster suffer like that? "Heyas!" I called out, making sure that my head was held high and that I strode as arrogantly down the baseline as if I owned the entire stadium. The pitcher would be watching me every second, I knew, and it was vital that he get the proper message from the very start of things.

Stealing bases was every bit as much a game of the mind as of the body, just like most of baseball. "How's tricks, Buster-Boy?"

"Cheetah!" he cried out in reply. For just a second his eyes widened in wonder at my new look, then he smiled just exactly the same way that he always did. It was impossible to dislike Buster, I suddenly realized, probably because he himself liked pretty much everyone else in the world. Which was just as well for me; the trait was why he was the one coach in baseball who didn't actively hate me. "Good to see you again, son. *Good* to see you!" His smile widened, then he turned to the would-be base-stealer. "Cheetah Jones, meet Thump Morris."

Thump's eyes widened; I thought it was the spot-thing at first but he never even mentioned it. "Jeez!" he exclaimed, taking my hand and shaking it enthusiastically. "I've seen so many of your game films! Buster shows them to me all the time."

I blushed a little, though of course no one but me could ever know it. "Really?"

"Uh-huh!" Thump continued, grinning like a kid. "You're *awesome*, man!"

"When he's not porking the manager's daughter in front of the press," Buster added sternly. "Or cussing out the fans. Or getting drunk on game days. Or. . ."

"Right, right, right," I countered. "There's no need to get into that. I'm sure he's heard the stories. Everyone else has." I held up my spotted arm. "And now there's this, too."

Thumps looked away. "They told us not to talk to you about that."

I blinked, then looked at Buster, who simply shrugged by way of an answer. "What's with that?" I asked. "I mean, we're a baseball team for christ's sake! We're gonna be living together for months!" I raised up my arm again. "How can we *not* talk about this?"

Buster grinned. "Your doc came and gave everyone a strict lecture. Coach Turnbull backed up every word. She said you're probably gonna have 'identity issues', whatever those are, and that everyone should give you a little space by not talking about it."

"She. . . I. . . Jeez!" I complained, turning away from Buster and looking around the field. Sure enough, everyone was staring at me. Though once they saw that I was looking back, everyone went right back to practicing as if nothing had happened. "I can't believe it. They went and messed up things even worse!"

"It's really all right," Thump explained. "No one's got a problem with it, I don't think. I mean, if a cheetah is who you really are, if that's your inner identity, well. . ." He smiled. "Who are we to complain? There's all sorts of strange people who play this game."

I turned to Buster. "Did he get that 'inner identity' baloney from Doctor Henway?"

He nodded silently.

"Jeez," I muttered again. After all, I couldn't tell anyone the *real* truth about why I was getting a morph-job. I'd known that going in. But the made-up story was even worse!

"Dancer Jenkins was especially supportive," Buster added, pointing towards right field. I followed his finger to where a player stood with his very long legs crossed, waiting for the little machine to loft him another fly ball. He saw me looking and gave me a furtive little grin and wave.

"Don't tell me. . ." I mumbled.

"Yep!" Buster replied. "You're absolutely right. Nothing wrong with your eyes at all, son! Like the kid said, all *sorts* of folks play this game." He grinned again. "And guess what! That little problem is all yours. I can't *wait* to see how you handle it!"

"Right," I murmured, looking over at the mound. *Gay exotic dancers*, I reminded myself. *That's who mostly has the fur thing done to them. Gay exotic dancers. . .*

The coach was done now with whatever he'd been telling his pitcher, and they were waiting for Buster and Thump. The right-hander was standing a little taller on the mound than he had been before, I noticed, and smirking just a tiny bit after having made

Thumps look so bad. "You know," I said slowly. "I'd like to take a crack at him."

"He's almighty fast!" Thumps warned me. "Reggie swivels like a big cat—"

"I've seen him," I interrupted.

Buster's eyes narrowed. "You ready to play yet?" he asked.

Clearly he hadn't gotten the word that I was supposed be taking things easy. Which meant that probably no one else out on the field had, either. "A little," I answered. "Until I get hot. My sweat glands are still all screwed up."

"Right," Buster answered, looking a little dubious. He eyed me up and down, then nodded. "If you want to run, run. I'm sure not going to be the one to stop you!"

Five minutes later, after doing some quick stretches, I was standing with my toe just barely touching first base, waiting for the pitcher to come to the set position. The first baseman, a big leftie who'd introduced himself simply as Steve, stood just behind me. But he wasn't important, not really. Not in this contest.

Instead, I locked my newly-yellow eyes onto the far more conventionally brown ones of young Reginald. It was already perfectly clear to both of us that we didn't like each other.

Not at all.

He toed the rubber, and I led off towards second. It was hot out in the sun; I could feel little streams of sweat flowing down my back under the fur. For a long time we stood immobile, neither giving a centimeter. Then he pivoted and fired. I made it look easy, coming back in standing up. He'd not shown his best, in turn I'd not moved my fastest. It was the nature of the game. Then Steve tossed the ball back to his pitcher, Reggie set up again, and I took six inches more lead than I had the first time.

Now! a little voice inside me screamed as big Reginald pivoted once more. He was smooth, all right. But not smoother than me! I came back into first on my belly this time, raising a little cloud of dust but once again easily safe. "Time!" I called, and Buster watched as I patted the dust first out of my uniform, and then out of my fur.

"That's gonna be a pain," he sympathized.

"I'll live," I muttered. "We'll work something out." Just then I had bigger fish to fry than the fur-thing. It was an offense against the natural order of the universe that a pitcher should be allowed to remain poised and confident with a man on first. Not even pitchers on my own team could be exempted from such a basic fact of existence. Once I was as brushed-off as possible I returned to the base, smiled real big at Reginald, and kicked my feet theatrically. Then, very carefully, I scratched my nose.

With my middle finger.

The pitcher's lips whitened. *Message received*, I noted. All was going according to plan.

"Time in!" Buster cried. I grinned towards the mound again. Once Reginald was set I led off just a little further than the previous two times. . .

. . .and then flew like the wind for second as Reginald pivoted and threw to Steve. Something was wrong with the throw, I knew from the way the kid had moved, though I couldn't have explained in a thousand years just *how* it was that I could tell. My heart pounded, my legs pumped, I filled my lungs once, twice, and then I was at second, with nary a shortstop nor second baseman in sight. The third-base coach was waving me on just as hard as he could, literally jumping and down in excitement, so I rounded the corner and pounded on with all I had. Then in a flash I was at third, sliding hard with my spikes riding up high and nasty. . .

. . .just as Steve emerged from the dugout with the ball that young, angry Reginald had so clearly just thrown there.

"T. . . T. . . Time!" I called again, and the beaming coach at third, whose name I still didn't even know yet, held up his arms and stopped play. Everyone on the field was staring at me, I suddenly realized, everyone on the damn team. Somewhere along the way they'd all stopped practice to watch the show. But they weren't staring at the spot-job anymore, or at least I didn't think so. Instead they were all grinning; Dancer was even jumping up and down and doing cheerleader kicks in a rather paisley sort of joy display. He must be a base-stealer too, I decided, to be so pleased with what I had just done; after all, with legs like those how could he *not* be?

Then the world began spinning around me, I sat down very hard on third base, and everything went black.

". . .shouldn't even be allowed back on the field!" the pitching coach was shouting at Tony, as I sat on the little bench beside my locker and allowed Herman to pour cold water over my head. "If youd'a seen it, Tony, I swear you'd feel the same way. It was a lousy *practice drill*, for crying out loud! Not guerrilla warfare!"

Young Reginald, I'd been told, hadn't been able to throw a single strike all afternoon once I'd finished with him. Apparently, I'd quite thoroughly rattled him. Such a pity, that.

"Now, Roger," Turnbull countered, a consoling note in his voice. "This is as close to the bigs as you can get without actually being there. Your kid is young. Too young, I think. We've been rushing him along ever since high school."

"Yeah!" the pitching coach answered, not sounding the least bit placated. "Because he's the hottest pitching prospect in our entire farm system! Or at least he was until that two-bit streetfighter of yours started screwing with his head!"

Suddenly Tony didn't sound happy. "Cheetah is *your* two-bit streetfighter too, Roger. Every bit as much as he is mine. We're all on the same team here. And don't you make a habit of forgetting it." There was a long silence. "The kid's going down to double-A tomorrow, Rog. Physically he's the hottest thing in the minors; I'll give you that. An arm like his doesn't come along once a decade. But he still has some growing up to do, which is right and natural at his age. This isn't the first time he's gone wild, not by a long shot." He sighed. "People are *going* to screw with his head, Roger. Can't you see that? Cheetah did his job out there today and did it well. If Reggie isn't grown up enough to play mind games and win, then he doesn't belong in triple-A ball. And that's that."

"Damn!" Roger declared, slamming his hat to the office floor. A long awkward moment passed, then the pitching coach bent over, picked up his headgear, and went storming down the hall towards the bullpen without so much as sparing me a glance.

"You feeling any better yet?" Herman asked after a few moments of silence had passed. He was smiling again, all happy wrinkles. The pitching staff had their own trainer, I knew. Which explained much.

"Yeah," I answered, even though my brain felt like it was about to explode. "Do I still have to go back to the hospital?"

"Nope," my trainer replied. "I managed to talk them out of it." Then the wrinkles hardened slightly. "But, you've got to stay out of the sun, Cheetah. For another week, at least."

I nodded. "Right." This time, I actually believed it.

"While you were out on the field," Herman continued, "I was doing some checking up. It seems that if we turn the air-conditioning down real low and also keep a close eye on your core-temperature, there's at least some workouts we can do right now."

"Really?" I asked. "Like what?"

Herman frowned. "I've been talking to Buster," he explained. "You're fast, Cheetah. And your glove is just fine at either shortstop or second. But you don't hit well for average."

I sighed and looked away as the water continued to trickle down my back. Wet fur smelled really, really bad, I decided. Though I was clearly going to have to get used to it. And it felt even worse, clammy and cold. "That's true," I admitted eventually. "It's not my fault. I've always been a weak hitter."

"Of course, it's not your fault," Herman replied reassuringly as he continued to dribble cold water over me from his big yellow sponge. "But I had an idea, see? And Buster likes it too. How about if we bulk you up a little?" I started to object, but before I could get the words out Herman was speaking again. "Just in the right places, not enough to slow you down. For example, bigger wrist muscles would give you more control of the bat. And improving your upper body strength in general could help you at the plate. You hit lots of grounders up the middle. With even just a little more zing on them, how many might dribble through and turn into singles? I think you could stand to carry a little more weight, so long as it's all muscle." He smiled again. "Besides, we can do extra speed-drills to make up for anything you might lose in that department. I've got some ideas that just might help there, too."

I frowned. *More* speed drills? And weightlifting too? "Look," I began slowly "That's a lot of work, probably all for nothing. I don't know if. . ."

"Great!" Herman replied as if I'd agreed with him. "I'm looking forward to spending a lot of time with you, then."

"He's bought into the new workout schedule?" a new voice boomed out from behind me; it was Tony, who'd apparently just then stepped out of his office to come and check up on me.

"Yep!" Herman agreed, squeezing his sponge over the top of my head so that for a moment I couldn't speak without getting sweaty-fur flavored water in my mouth. "He seems real enthusiastic about the whole thing, Coach. Just like Buster told me he'd be."

"Hmm," Turnbull muttered, his tone dubious. He bent over and, squinting his eyes, examined me like a rancher looking over a prime beef. "Well. Whaddaya know?"

Then he was gone.

***

The next few weeks were absolute misery.

My body changes should've been the worst of it. Yes, the paw-pads did in fact begin to grow in, just as promised, on both my hands and my feet. But the damned things itched like the devil, all day long and into the night. Doctor Henway gave me some cream to rub into them. It stopped the itching, sure enough. But the stuff also stank, so badly that no one would willingly sit downwind of me. Even worse, I was told, I'd soon need to rub the same ointment into my lips and nose. How I'd ever manage to tolerate *that* was beyond me!

I'd asked Buster to find me a place to stay before going into the hospital. He came up with a nice apartment, located in a clean little complex within a short drive of the field. I couldn't really complain, considering he'd also loaned me enough money to pay my first month's share of the rent. And it would've been ungrateful to do so anyway, because it really *was* such a nice little place. Still, Thumps was not at all whom I'd have freely chosen as a roommate. It wasn't that there was anything to dislike about him; far from it. But jeez! He was so, like. . .

. . .wholesome.

"I've got to go, Mom," he was saying into his phone as he opened the door for me the very first time. "My new apartment mate is here." A pause, while he smiled apologetically at me. Thumps wasn't more than four years younger than me, yet he seemed like such a little kid! "Yes, Mom, I know him pretty well. He's on the team with me, remember?" Then there was other pause, as Thumps rolled his eyes theatrically. "Mom and Dad are coming by next weekend," he explained, placing his hand over the mouthpiece. "and Mom wants to know if cannelloni is okay for dinner? With steamed broccoli?"

Inside my purported home I felt like I was living in a doll-house. Thumps was neat, almost compulsively so, and it was nerve-wracking in the extreme to have him constantly chasing around after me closing cabinet doors and picking things up. He never uttered a word of complaint about my slovenliness, which actually made things worse. Thumps was a good kid, maybe even a great kid. Which was precisely why he made me so uncomfortable. I mean, he didn't even *drink*!

Practice wasn't any fun either. I didn't mind batting practice, or fielding practice, or even a few wind sprints considering my specialty. But Herman, I'd decided, was trying to *kill* me! No sooner was I done with the weight machine then he wanted me to sprint like a maniac through his special course, where I had to place my feet in painted boxes and lift my knees high. Then I did squats and lifted dumbells until the cows came home, long after everyone else on the team had gone.

All except for Dancer and Thumps, of course. Impressed by my first-day showing, they'd decided to adopt my new training regimen, too. So I was never left alone to suffer in peace. Instead of just me and my trainer, I was stuck with having two fellow players at my elbow all of the time. It wouldn't have been so bad, except that Dancer was easily stronger than I was. And, worst of all, Thumps was always a tick or two faster every time we raced. I'd never, *ever* been on a team with someone faster than me before. It was a lot harder to take than I'd have expected. Every time he beat me to second base I wanted to grab the little jerk by the throat and throttle the life out of him. Then, I had to go home and eat his mom's leftover cannelloni.

At least having Dancer stay over with us meant that Thumps and I got a ride to and from the field. I couldn't afford a car, and rather to my shock Thumps had never learned to drive. Dancer's life-partner Dasher (people always called him that, and he seemed to like it well enough) had an old beat-up sedan, so we always had wheels.

Did I mention that Dancer and Dasher lived directly upstairs over us? My teammate had earned his nickname fair and square, it seemed. Every morning, just after the break of dawn, he began his daily routine by performing classical ballet in his living room. "It's *great* for balance!" he'd explained to me the first day, "And for agility and flexibility, too! You could work out with us anytime you liked!" He looked pretty hurt when I explained that things weren't necessarily as they might appear about me, despite the fact that I was as gentle as possible about it.

After all, I needed his wheels.

Plus, when I wasn't doing ten-thousand dumbbell lifts or sprinting like a fool around the basepads I was back at the hospital having tests run. It was absolutely essential that the team be able to prove at a moment's notice that none of my modifications were performance-enhancing in any way, and that my athletic abilities were still limited by the same natural factors that they'd always been. So, I spent hours patiently enduring electrical stimulation of my nerves and muscles, bright flashes in my dilated eyes, and a thousand other torments from the innermost circles of hell. Sometimes Dr. Henway came to look me over and made little cosmetic adjustments here and there to keep things under control. In truth, I had to give her credit. Even with my face still looking all funny from the long whiskers that didn't really belong without a muzzle, I couldn't help but find my new self considerably more attractive than the old. Instead of looking gaunt and haunted, I now came across as lean and determined.

The absolute worst, though, was the shrink. I didn't understand what was up with that from the very beginning; all we ever talked about was how things had been when I was growing up. One session we talked about how Mom's boyfriends had beaten me up so often, another time about when I'd come home from ball practice and found her overdosed on the couch. I'd had to call an ambulance, and she'd nearly died anyway. "Why did you work so hard at baseball?" Dr. Forster asked me one day. "When you had so much else going on in your life?"

I shrugged, then frowned at myself for having done so; the gesture had felt childish, somehow. "I dunno. It was just there."

My shrink nodded and smiled. An endless silence ensued while I sat and thought. Jeez, how should I know why I did anything? "I was good at it," I answered finally.

Dr. Foster smiled and once again said nothing. More accursed silence.

"It was, like, the only thing that meant anything to me," I explained so as to fill the aching emptiness. "The only thing that felt good. Mom was a piece of garbage, her lovers even worse. . ." I frowned, a little surprised at how angry I was suddenly getting. "No one ever gave a damn about anything I did. Except the coaches."

"They spent a lot of time with you, I'd imagine."

"Heck, yeah! I was always, like, the whole team. Best hitter, best pitcher, best runner. . . I was their ticket to bigger and better things."

This time Dr. Forster frowned. "So, it was Cheetah Jones the player you felt they really cared about, then? Not Cheetah Jones the growing young man?"

"Heh!" I barked, leaning back and folding my arms. "Let me tell you something, Mr. Headshrinker! Back then, I was the genuine item! I carried our team to the state championship not once but twice, and everyone knew it. No one cared if I sold a little weed for pocket change or cut a few classes, if you know what I mean. No one! Not even the friggin' principal!"

"I see," Dr. Forster replied mildly. "I think I really am indeed beginning to see."

All the sessions were like that, really. One time I asked the old man if we were ever gonna talk about me growing fur. "Would you like to talk about the fur?" he'd asked in return, and I just about wept in frustration. What was I wasting time in therapy for, anyway? Didn't I have enough to deal with, what with the extra training and all that? All it ever did was stir me up; I always left all mad about stuff that had happened years ago. And why couldn't Buster have roomed me up with someone who at least kept a few cold beers in his fridge, like any normal human being? Why?

Worst of all, if I had to listen to Swan Lake at five in the morning even one more time my head was gonna explode!

7

The best thing about spring training is that it eventually ends. The winners get to stay up with the team, the losers get shipped down a level, and finally everyone gets to play real baseball games instead of stupid simulations. Dancer, Thumps and I all easily made the cut. I hit leadoff and played short, Thumps moved over to second from his natural position of short to accommodate me and batted in the number-two spot, Dancer batted third and played left field, while Pudge Hiller hit cleanup and caught most days. The idea was that if one or two of us fast-movers could get on base, then all sorts of good things could begin happening all at the same time. With a base-stealer on, for example, Pudge would be certain to come up to bat in his number four spot. The threat to steal might unbalance the pitcher enough, say, to hang a curve ball for Pudge. With his bat, one hung curve was all he needed to put a couple runs onto the scoreboard. Alternatively, the stress of facing Pudge might make the pitcher forget about the runners on base, allowing them to steal at will so that a mere single or sacrifice fly might bring them home. Plus, having all three speedsters in the top of the order put a huge stress on the opposing lineup's fielders; if they made the slightest mistake in ball-handling we'd eat their lunch on the basepads. And even worse they knew it and would fret about it, sometimes even for days in advance. So, working together, we hoped to induce a lot of fielding errors. The rest of the lineup was mediocre at best, though we had an outstandingly good pitching staff for a minor league team. I'd once heard Coach Turnbull claim that he'd traded half a team's worth of prospects for Pudge Hiller, and the evidence was clear to see in the rest of our lineup. We four top-of-the-order types would either score enough runs to carry the team or else we wouldn't. It was just that simple. On us, and on the pitchers, rested the fate of the entire club.

The press seemed to know it, too. All four of us had been getting interview requests every day for weeks. The other three had been talking to the reporters for ages now, but so far I hadn't. Our opening game was at home, and after our last pre-season practice Tony called me into his office for a private talk. "I can't tell you anymore how you ought to handle the press," he explained. "So far, I've ordered you to stay away from them and I'll give you full credit for obeying instructions. You're looking pretty fair out on the ballfield, too. Working hard, even. And it shows." He folded his arms and leaned back in his sweat-stained swivel chair. "Eventually, though, you've gotta grow up. You want to talk to them, you've got the green light. You don't, I'll keep 'em off your back. Whaddaya want to do?"

I frowned for just an instant, then winced and flattened out my mouth again. It hurt to frown; perhaps my muzzle was starting to come in? "My agent says that I ought to make friends with them," I said slowly. "To spread my name out as far and wide as I possibly can. That's the way to get sponsorships."

Tony nodded slowly, but remained silent.

"On the other hand," I continued, "what have reporters ever really done for me except get me into trouble? All they are is a pain in the butt." I sighed, then shook my head. "You know, I haven't done a thing but play baseball ever since I got here. Not a single thing!"

My coach nodded his head again.

"Play baseball, run sprints, work out until the cows come home. . ." I tried to frown again, being a slow learner. It hurt even worse the second time. "Plus turn into a friggin' cheetah. Jesus Christ!" Finally, I shook my head and opened the office door. "Tell the reporters to stay away, Coach. Only pretty it up some, willya? I've got enough on my plate just now without them."

* * * *

Opening Day was an impressive event, for a minor-league operation. A bunch of local business leaders turned out for the Monday afternoon game, and the franken-plant factory actually shut down their smelliest operations as a favor for us, so that we weren't half-choking for once. The stands were almost two-thirds full, an outstanding turnout for AAA ball. I broke a shoelace just before the Star-Spangled Banner began to play and went jogging down to my locker to pick up a spare.

"Hey!" Tony cried out as soon as he saw me, banging on his office window. "Hey, Cheetah!"

"Hi, Coach!" I answered, smiling slightly. Everyone was wondering where Tony was. Most of us figured he was in the crapper; the rumor was that he'd eaten half a ton of jambalaya the night before at some kind of season-opening dinner.

He banged the window again. "Cheetah!" he demanded. "Get over here!"

I wasn't really supposed to be in the clubhouse so close to game-time and I knew it. But I had a perfectly good reason; surely Tony would understand! "I've got a broken shoelace," I explained, holding up my foot so that he could see the dangling end. "I'm trying to get fixed up before the first pitch. See? It's not my fault."

"Damnit!" Tony roared. "I don't care about your shoelace! Get over here! My door is stuck; I think the lock is broken."

My jaw dropped for just an instant, then I jogged across and around. "Grab the other side," Tony directed. "See if you can help me force it. I've got our lineup card in here with me!"

We yanked and pulled and shook together but got nowhere. "Damnit!" Tony roared. "Go get Herman! And tell Buster, too!"

Presently everyone and their brother was standing around Tony's office while he raved and cursed and threw things. "Opening day!" he roared out. "Opening damn day! I'm the laughingstock of the league!"

"It's okay, Tony," the opposing coach reassured him. They were old friends, having played together for a few years back in the day. "Look at the bright side. With a half-animal playing short and a flamer in left field you'd have been the laughingstock anyhow."

"Probably," the chief umpire agreed, smirking. He was holding the game up until Tony could be freed.

"Let me try," Pudge Hiller suggested, holding up a bat. "Maybe I can knock the knob clean off." Everyone backed off a little, then Pudge raised his weapon and brought it down with all the hard, trained muscle of a professional power-hitter behind the blow.

Wham! the bat went as it slammed into the knob. . .

. . .which sheared off clean, ricocheted hard off of the cement floor, then flew back up and hit Pudge square in the face. "Damn!" the big man moaned, dropping his bat and bending over double.

"Damn!" Tony echoed from inside his little prison. He tried the door again; it was still just as stuck as before. "Damn, damn, damn!"

"Let me through!" Herman cried out, forcing his way to the front of the crowd. Pudge was sort of rocking back and forth now, moaning. Ominously, blood was trickling down the back of his hands.

"Damn!" Tony repeated himself, seeing the bleeding. "What a stupid, idiotic way to. . ."

"It's *all right*," Herman interrupted, sidling up to Pudge's side and staring daggers at Tony. "Everything's going to be perfectly all right. Here, Pudge. Let's get your hands down so we can take a good look at that face of yours. . ."

Just then, with perfect timing, the stadium loudspeakers came to life. "Attention, ladies and gentlemen! Your attention, please! Is there a locksmith in the house. . ."

***

It was just as well that we won the opening game; had we not I fear that Tony might've done something foolish. Buster had been forced to rush Pudge to the hospital for x-rays and then a proton-scan, but despite a truly nasty bruise on his cheek and a gash that took seven stitches to repair no serious damage was done. Still, no one at the ballpark knew for sure that he was okay until the bottom of the fourth, and by then we had well and truly gone to town on our arch-rival Grenada Muskrats. I went three for four with two stolen bases, Dancer hit what by rights should've been a double but which his long legs stretched into a triple, and Thumps walked twice while I distracted the pitcher out on the basepads. Even gray-haired old Pudge Jefferson put on a show; he hit two homers for no less than five RBI's, looking fifteen years younger as he limped across home plate for the second time in one afternoon.

But the magic couldn't last forever. Soon Dancer was struggling at the plate and the elder Pudge's gimpy knees were keeping him from running out singles. Even worse, Thumps never really got started; we were into the third week before he quit being zip for the season at the plate. He took more and more batting practice, but just couldn't seem to connect. I was feeling plenty sorry for him, just like everyone else. But what can one player do for another when he's in a slump? I left him in Buster's capable hands and tried not to make too big a mess back at the apartment.

Things might've sucked for the team as a whole, but personally I was living high and wide. At least I was hitting all right, even if no one else was. Plus, I was stealing bases. A few fans were beginning to show up wearing cheetah-spotted hats and sometimes even makeup jobs. If I got stranded all of the time instead of being driven home to score, was that my fault? What could I do about other people's problems?

Once I got a few full paychecks in and had paid off the especially angry collection agencies, I was finally able to buy a few nice things for myself. Thumps had furnished the apartment, so there wasn't any need for anything along those lines. So I went down to the mall and priced myself out a big, heavy gold chain just like the one I'd treated myself to when I'd first broken through into the majors, then had pawned in the Dominican Republic for airfare back home. But when I tried it on in the store, my fur kept getting caught in all the little links. It hurt whenever I moved. Finally, I gave up on the whole thing as a bad idea.

My credit rating might be nothing more than a fond memory, but I still had a nice roll of bills burning a hole in my pocket. So I went down and bought myself an alcohol-powered scooter to run back and forth to the field with, and maybe to get around town when it wasn't raining. Dancer and Dasher were bickering all of the time about another man that Dasher might or might not be seeing, and riding with them had definitely ceased to be fun. Sure, a better ride would've been nicer. But given a choice between the kind of piece of junk car I could afford to pay cash for and a brand-new scooter that would actually start when I pressed the button, I felt like I made a pretty good deal. Pretty soon I was zipping all around Baton Rouge. Buster looked a little worried when I first showed up on the thing, but Tony never complained; he had plenty of other stuff on his mind. Plus, I suspect, Thumps was probably glad to be rid of me from time to time. "How do you read the pitchers so well?" he was constantly asking me. "Do you keep a book? This guy Hastings who's pitching tomorrow; have you ever seen him play before?" It was all baseball, baseball, baseball with Thumps; between his continual nagging and the ongoing ballet recital upstairs a man couldn't get any rest! It was a good thing that our division was mostly concentrated in the delta country; at least our bus rides tended to be short and we weren't often on the road for more than a week or two at a time.

Things got even worse when Pudge Hiller came back off of the disabled list. Everyone expected that his power at the plate would give the team a big lift. But it didn't work out that way at all. *Whoof! Whoof! Whoof!* his bat would go, and our finest hitter was down on strikes. Something seemed to be really bothering the man. "Heya, Cheetah," he mumbled glumly sometimes in passing; more often he said nothing at all. If he'd smiled once since spring training, no one had caught him in the act. But I had my own problems.

Most of them were with my shrink. "What do you feel when you look into the mirror these days?" he asked me one week, not too terribly long before mid-season. We were eight games under five-hundred, and nearly in last place. Even worse, I'd gone nothing for three at the plate that afternoon and made an error in the field. And now here I was, having to talk about feelings. Talk about a miserable day!

"Like I'm a real dork," would've been an honest answer; things were getting to the point where it was hard to see the old Cheetah behind the new. Sometimes it felt like I was wearing a mask that wouldn't come off, and somehow that really bothered me. I was having freaky dreams, too. My muzzle was beginning to grow in, and I missed three days while I had a bunch of old teeth pulled and new, more ferocious ones implanted. I repeatedly bit the inside of my cheeks for a week afterwards, which was even worse than my itchy tattoo had been. On top of that, the base of my spine was continually burning where my tail was about to emerge. "I feel just the same way as I always did," I answered instead.

"And how is that?" Forster asked.

Jesus! Would *nothing* satisfy the man? "Like I'm looking at me," I explained. "Like, I'm checking to see if there's a speck of dirt in my eye or something." My eyes narrowed; I was growing tired of this game. "How do *you* feel when you look in the mirror, doc?"

"Like I could stand to lose fifty pounds," he answered, grinning his most annoying grin. "Do your teammates seem to treat you any differently?"

I shrugged. "They hardly ever speak to me at all anymore."

The shrink's eyebrows rose. "Really?"

"Yeah," I agreed, shifting a little in my seat. Dr. Forster had been nice enough to find one that was kind to my tail-issues, but with all the swelling I still wasn't very comfortable. "That's how it always is, though. I don't think it's because of the fur."

"You're a loner, then?"

I nodded. "Pretty much. When you stay off to yourself, people don't keep asking you to do things for them, see? You leave them alone, they leave you alone. No one gets hurt."

"When you get close to people, they hurt you?"

"Usually," I answered, wriggling uncomfortably again.

"Do you have any friends at all?" Dr. Forster asked.

I shrugged. "I live with Thumps. He's all right, I guess. Though he's a pest sometimes. It used to really piss me off."

"He bothers you?"

"Yeah," I answered, curling my lip slightly in disgust. It looked a lot better with the new teeth. "At first he was always asking for advice. Like, how far to lead off first. Or how to mind-game a pitcher." I frowned. "He irritated me all through spring training, and even for a little while after. But now it's finally slacked off some."

"Uh-huh," Dr. Forster said, smiling encouragingly.

"He followed me around like a little kid," I continued, my frown intensifying. "I'm glad he's past that."

Dr. Forster frowned, then hesitated a minute as if he were thinking about something. "You mentioned to me once that you had a younger brother," he said slowly.

I felt my lip curl still further, into a definite snarl. "What about him?"

"Well. . ." Forster smiled. "People are generally pretty close to their brothers. Yet I don't recall your ever mentioning his name. Have you seen him lately? Are you close? How does he feel about the 'fur thing', as you call it?"

I sat still for a little while, until the cramps from my suddenly-balled fists became painful. Then, very slowly, I climbed to my feet and stood towering over my shrink. "I don't want to talk to you about my brother," I said very slowly. "Not now or ever in the future. Do you understand me?"

Forster visibly paled. "I. . . I mean. . . Cheetah. . ."

I shook my head. "Doc, I'll talk to you about baseball all you want. I'll tell you everything you want to hear about my reflection in the mirror. I agreed to talk to you about that kind of thing, and I'll keep my word. But don't you *ever* bring up my younger brother again. He ain't got nothin' to do with anything. You hear me?"

Forster nodded, sweating visibly. "I. . . I. . ."

"Good," I answered, turning to leave even though the session wasn't half over. "I'll see you next Tuesday."

8

I nearly wrecked my scooter three times on the way home that afternoon; twice when I entered curves way too fast and once when I cut in front of a delivery truck with bad brakes. My hands were still shaking with rage when I pulled up in front of Thumps' and my little apartment. I lowered the sidestand with a savage kick, took off my helmet, and then headed up the sidewalk. Damn, but I needed a drink!

"Hey, Cheetah!" a voice called out from behind me. It was Buster, climbing out of his old Cadillac halfway across the lot. "Wait up!"

I closed my eyes and sighed. What else could possibly go wrong today? "Sure," I answered, allowing a little of my anger make itself heard in my tone.

Buster came bustling up, then eyed me up and down nervously. "Are you all right?" he asked.

"Well enough," I answered. "What gives?"

He frowned, then looked away. "I've got a situation, Cheetah," he explained. "A bad one. And I could use some help."

I felt my ears stir slightly. It felt. . . odd. "What kind of situation?"

"I'm not entirely sure yet," he explained, meeting my eyes once more. "Truth be told, I came to see if I could get Dancer to come with me. But when I got up close to the door, I could hear him and Dasher fighting again."

I nodded. "They've been at it for weeks."

"Yeah," he agreed, looking at the ground again. "I know."

"What about Thumps?" I asked, pointing at our window. "He could help you."

Buster shook his head. "No, I don't think so." Once again, he met my eyes. "Cheetah, the fact is that things might get rough, see? And though I think the world of the kid most ways, Thumps isn't exactly who I'd want covering my back in a fight. Not that he wouldn't give his best, mind you. But. . ."

I nodded, intrigued despite myself. "Yeah. No street smarts." I paused and pressed my lips together, then nodded my head. "All right, Buster. I reckon I owe you one. Maybe even more than one. So let's go take care of this, whatever it is. But can you at least let me know what I'm getting myself into?"

****

". . .been coming in every day with bruises," Buster explained as he drove us across town. "Not really bad ones, mind you. But enough to make Herman wonder."

I nodded. "Uh-huh."

"He's in a terrible slump," Buster continued. "Anyone can see there's something wrong with Pudge." He sighed. "When *you* don't talk to anyone, Cheetah, that's normal. But ever since his first couple of weeks, Pudge has clammed up too."

I shrugged. There were terrible bags under our star catcher's eyes of late. "Sometimes he really looks like he's at the end of his rope." Then I frowned. "But look, Buster. Pudge is a huge, powerful man. If he's got bruises on him I'd hate to see the other guy."

Buster nodded. "I know. Which is part of why this is all so strange." He frowned. "I tried to call his house tonight. Someone answered, but then all I heard was yelling before I got cut off. It sounded pretty ugly. Expect anything."

"Gotcha." I curled my lip and looked out the window. We were in the older part of town now, where the lots were large and well-manicured. Our catcher made more money than any of the rest of us, and therefore could well afford to live in such a nice area. He was married, though his wife never came out to the field to see him. None of us had met her at all, that I knew of.

Buster made two more lefts down quiet, residential streets, then a right into a long, magnolia-lined gravel driveway. The instant the car stopped we could hear shouting.

"Damn you!" a female voice was shrieking. "Can't you do anything right? Move it back this way again."

"Honey," Pudge's voice answered, a little unsteady. "It's awfully heavy. Why can't we. . ."

Whap! Something hit something else, hard. "Ow!" Pudge objected. "Kathy, please! You don't—"

WhapWhapWhap! "Pick it up, you miserable bastard!"

I looked over at Buster, who was already looking at me. "Jeez," he muttered.

"Yeah," I agreed.

Buster went directly to the front door, while I sort of sidled off towards an open window. Sure enough, just across the room Pudge was bent over a heavy-looking dresser while his wife beat him about the head and shoulders with what looked like a curtain rod. "You. . . Stupid. . . Idiot!" she declared, punctuating each word with a blow. "You're fat! And useless! And stupid! And. . ."

"Honey!" Pudge answered, falling to his knees under the rain of blows. It was ridiculous in a way; the young giant could easily have turned around and killed his wife with one hand tied behind his back. Yet at the same time it was also touching. Clearly, he was trying his best to make things work. "I love you, honey! Ow! Please, put that down and let's. . . Ow! Honey, remember what the counselor. . ."

"To hell with the counselor!" she declared, redoubling the intensity of her attack. "And to hell with *you!*" I felt my lip curl back again; there was *something* about what I was looking at. I couldn't quite put my finger on it, but it bothered me.

A lot.

Just then the doorbell rang and Kathy threw down her weapon in disgust. "I'll be right back!" she declared. "And we'll see then if you can put something *exactly* where you're told to!"

Then she was gone, and Pudge was bent over the dresser, sobbing. "Psst!" I said. "Over here!" I scratched at the window screen.

Pudge raised his head. "Who. . ."

"It's me!" I explained. "Cheetah! And that's Buster at the front door,"

He turned towards me and I saw that his face was a mass of

bruises. "Cheetah? What. . ."

"Come on!" I ordered. "Open the window!"

"Open the window?" he repeated, looking baffled.

Well. . . Maybe he was stunned from the beating, I reasoned. "Come *on*!" I hissed. "We're getting you out of here. Now!"

"But. . . But. . ."

I snarled, then punched out the screen. "Come *on*!" I ordered, extending a spotted hand. "Buster and I will find a place to put you up. We've *got* to get you out of here."

Pudge frowned. "Cheetah," he said slowly, "I know you mean well. But Kathy's just a little hot-tempered. She loves me, deep down inside, and—"

"Baloney!" I declared. I'd heard enough of this same sort of crap from my Mom, usually while I was holding an ice bag to either her battered face or my own. I tore the screen open wider. "Get out here, Pudge. We haven't got all night."

"Cheetah, I. . . Uh. . ."

"Damn it!" I declared, pounding the windowsill. "If you don't get your butt out here, I'll tell every reporter in the world that your real name is Adolph!"

Pudge's jaw worked slowly once, then twice. "Cheetah, you bastard—"

"I'll do it!" I shrieked. "I'm just the man for the job! And you know it!"

The catcher's jaw worked one last time, then he bared his teeth at me. "You are, aren't you? You miserable jackass!"

I took one step back and smiled wide, letting the pointy teeth show. "Try me."

All of this time Buster and Kathy had been shouting at each other through the front door; it now slammed. "Time's up, Adolph!" I declared.

"Damn!" he hissed through clenched teeth. "Damn, damn, damn!"

Then, to my intense relief, he climbed through the window and dropped heavily to the ground beside me. "Come on!" I urged, pointing. "Buster's car is right over there."

9

Things were pretty much back to normal by morning, at least on the surface. We woke up again to Swan Lake, car-pooled to the field and worked out. The division-leading Muskrats were back in town, and rather to our surprise we shellacked them. I led off with a ground-rule double, stole third and scored when Thumps, for once, delivered a perfect sacrifice fly. Then things *really* broke lose when Pudge Hiller got to the plate. Buster had urged him to sit the game out; he'd been up half the night icing down his bruises and explaining to the police that no, he did *not* wish to press spousal-abuse charges against his wife. The Muskrat pitcher made the mistake of confusing Pudge's obvious fatigue for weak resolve and challenged him with a fastball right down central. Our catcher drilled it far over the center-field wall, so hard that it was still rising when it left the stadium. After that all we did all evening long was run up the score. I hit for the cycle, including my first honest-to-goodness over-the-wall home run as a professional. (I'd hit an inside-the-park one during my brief stint in the bigs, but somehow that didn't feel like it counted.) Everywhere I looked, cheetah-print hats were flying in the air. My bulging muscles were beginning to pay off. That night Mr. Sandrell called me up to congratulate me; "Cheetah," he said, "I'm very pleased with your performance so far. It makes me believe in the magic of baseball more than ever." I couldn't believe that he'd actually *noticed*, much less taken the time to call.

But even that wasn't the most memorable event of the day. After the phone call Coach Turnbull stopped by my locker. "You and I have something we need to do when you're out of the shower," he said shortly. "Out in the business office." Then he was gone.

I wondered what it was about the whole time I washed up. I'd stayed clean, hadn't I? Not a single beer had passed my lips in weeks, though at times it'd been hard, hard, hard. My personal numbers were plenty good, even if the team was nine and a half back. That wasn't *my* fault! I hadn't given a single interview to anyone. . . So, what was his complaint? And why the business office instead of his usual haunt down by the locker room?

It took me all of half a second to figure things out when I burst unannounced through Turnbull's office door. He was behind his desk. . .

. . .and sitting across from him was the wheelchair-kid we'd run into in New York. . . What was his name?

"You may remember Raymond," my coach began, forestalling any difficulties. "And his mother, Mrs. Belanger."

I smiled and nodded, then awkwardly removed my hat. He still weirded me out, though I did my best not to let it show. Weirded me out, and something more. Though I wasn't sure quite what. "Hi," was all I said.

"I just wanted to thank you for the picture," young Raymond said, his voice thin and weak. He didn't look nearly so good as he had in front of the Freedom Center, and that hadn't been all that great. "It was so cool!"

"We're down here visiting my in-laws," Mrs. Belanger explained with a smile. "Once we found out where you played, well. . ."

I smiled and nodded, then squatted down alongside the wheelchair. "It was a pleasure. Though, that pic is a wee bit. . . Outdated."

"Yeah!" Raymond agreed, eyes large. "It sure is!" Then he smiled again. "You hit for the cycle. It was so cool!"

I'd do it again, I heard a little voice say in the back of my head, *a thousand times over, if it could do a damn thing to help you.* "Not nearly so cool as seeing you again," I said instead. Then I turned to Coach Turnbull. "I presume you have the latest version handy?"

He smiled and passed it over. "To Raymond," I signed it, trying not to cry. Why was this kid getting to me so badly, all of a sudden? "Who believed in me."

"Gosh!" he said when I handed it over.

"Gosh," I repeated. Then I looked over at the coach again, eyes brimming with tears. "Is this the best we can do?"

Turnbull blinked, genuinely caught off guard. "No. Of course not." He got out his little pad and scribbled. "Mrs. Belanger," he explained, "If you'd simply have let us know that you were in town, you'd have watched the game from the dugout. Just like Boston."

"Wow!" Raymond gasped.

"In fact," he continued, still scribbling, "You two can watch any game you please from our dugout, from here onwards. We're officially adopting you. Or else they can fire me if they'd rather; I don't give a sh. . . er, darn. And, if you'll let us know ahead of time that you're coming, every player on the team will sign a baseball for you, right in front of your eyes." He tore off the paper and handed it to Mrs. Belanger. "If you'd like, I can also try and arrange for a benefit game. For the Cancer Society, I mean."

"That. . . That. . ." she stuttered. A single tear ran down her cheek.

"Wow!" Raymond gushed. I was wearing shorts; he reached out with one arm and hugged my spotted leg. "I always *knew* you were all right! No matter what anyone else said."

"I'm not all right, really," I admitted, my voice thick with emotion. "I'm actually a pathetic jackass. But. . . But. . ." Then I shook my head, smiled, patted Raymond on the head. . .

. . .and got out of there quick before I broke down blubbering in front of them.

***

In some ways it was tough being the only success story on the entire team. I didn't get along well with other people even under the best of circumstances. But now, with me developing my own personal fanbase and reporters coming from all over the world to watch and photograph me play in fur even though they knew I wouldn't grant them an interview, well. . . I was more a loner than ever. About the only time anyone ever came to talk to me was the night that Pudge Hiller showed up at the apartment after a game and asked me to come outside so he could speak to me in private. Once we were alone together he extended his hand. "I'm sorry I called you a jackass," he said.

"When did you do that?" I demanded.

He reddened. "Back at my house. The night that. . . that. . ."

"Oh!" I answered, smiling and accepting his hand without reservation. "Don't worry about it. You were. . ." My voice trailed off, for lack of words.

"Yeah," he agreed. "I was." Then he looked off into the distance. "I also want to thank you for how you've handled the whole situation. Not just for forcing me to make the break, though for that alone I owe you plenty. But also for keeping your mouth shut ever since. I mean. . ."

I smiled back, then held up a furry arm. "I live in a glass house," I explained softly. "Thank you, and the rest of the team, for giving me so little grief over *this*."

"Heh!" He grinned. "Behind your back, I. . . We. . ." He colored again, then shook his head. "You're our star player," he said finally. "How much can we. . ."

"Right," I agreed into the sudden silence. Somehow I felt better, knowing that people were laughing at me. Though exactly *why* the knowledge made me feel better I'd never figure out no matter how long I lived. "I understand."

"I've filed for divorce," he continued. "I plan to start all over again, or at least as near to it as I can manage. Begin a whole new life. But before I could even start I had to make sure you knew how very grateful I am, to you and Buster both." His hand reached out again, and I shook it a second time.

"Don't mention it," I repeated.

"If there's anything I can ever do. . ."

"There *is* something," I said softly into the moonlight.

"What's that?" he asked.

"Get mad, Pudge," I urged him. "You play your best ball when you're angry, just like I do. We're more alike than you think, down under the skin. Don't put up with anyone else's garbage like that ever again, on the field or off. I don't, and you shouldn't have to either."

The big Kentuckian blinked in the darkness. "You know what?" he said softly. "I think you just may have something there."

10

We were scheduled to hit the road the next day for our longest scheduled trip of the year, to Jacksonville, Roswell, Raleigh and Grenada. Because the bus was leaving at one I had to see the shrink early in the morning. It didn't seem to matter much; he was still the same stubborn idiot he'd always been, turning everything back on me. This time, though, I surprised him by opening up with a question. "Can this cheetah stuff change who I am inside?" I demanded.

The doctor tilted his head first to one side, then the other. "Not in any direct sense, no," he answered.

I shook my head angrily. "Don't weasel-word me," I countered. Then I pointed to my head. "I've been living inside here for as long as I can remember. And things are getting all *different* now."

"Different how?" he asked, blinking behind his dark-rimmed glasses.

I shook my head. "Like. . . There's this kid, see? He's sick. I should be charging him for autographs, but I'm not. Even though I'm perfectly entitled and not exactly rolling in the dough. And there's Thumps. . . He's our second baseman and my room-mate. The one who's always bothering me with questions."

The doctor nodded, but said nothing.

"I should've bitten his head off a long time ago; he's *fast*, and like as not someday he'll be trying to take my position away from me. But all the time we were in the dugout yesterday I was showing him how to read a pitcher better. That's *stupid* of me; I shouldn't be doing *that*! And then a little while back Buster and me helped another player run away from his wife; she was beating him, you see. Her beating *him*, and she maybe half his size! I shoulda doubled over laughing. Instead we got him out, and he came by my place last night to thank me for doing it. And upstairs there's the biggest comedy opera in history playing itself out; two flamers who dress up in tights and dance *ballet* every morning, for God's sake! They're fighting now, and instead of busting a gut over it I'm laying awake at night worrying that they're gonna break up!"

The doctor stared at me for a long time, not the way he usually did when he was trying to bore me into talking, but rather like he was for-real thinking about something. Then he spoke aloud. "Your brother," he said at last. "You said he was younger than you. Was he a *lot* younger, maybe? And abused even worse than you were? Maybe even sexually?"

My mouth dropped open, revealing newly-fierce teeth. Then an icy rage closed in over my heart. "You. . ." I began, feeling still-unfamiliar claws digging into my pawpads. "You. . ."

Then the doctor sighed and leaned back. "I'm sorry," he said. "You told me that you didn't want to discuss your brother, and that's certainly your right. I should never have brought the subject up. It clearly has nothing whatsoever to do with your cheetah-job, which is the only treatment you've signed up for." He smiled, icy-cold. "No, of *course* growing a fur coat can't change who you are inside. Your brain hasn't been altered at all, except in that the binge-drinking damage is responding well to treatment. If you feel different now about yourself and those around you, well. . . I'm afraid that you'll have to look elsewhere for the reason why."

I was still all pissed off about the shrink when I swung my scooter into the apartment lot. Because it was going to be such a long road trip there weren't to be any workouts. All we had to do was get to the stadium by one. I was all packed and ready, not having much stuff to worry about in the first place. But on the way back to the apartment Dasher's wildly-driven car nearly ran me off the road, and when I got home there was Dancer, still in his morning ballet getup, weeping his eyes out on the parking lot. It didn't take a genius to put two and two together. I *could* have walked right past him. But, somehow, I didn't. "Come on," I urged the left-fielder, taking him by the shoulder and physically turning him around towards the building. "It's all over now."

"I. . . I found someone's pants," he explained. "They. . . They weren't—"

"I know," I interrupted, not really wanting to hear the details. "Come on. Let's get inside and then we can talk." I put my arm around his shoulders, and with an audible sob of relief he sort of melted into my fur-job. *What in the world are you **doing**?* the little voice in my head screamed. *People are gonna **see** this, man!* But for some odd reason Buster's face flashed into my mind for a moment and I refused to pull away.

"We were supposed to be for *life!*" Dancer wailed. "I don't know. . . I mean. . ."

People *were* staring, it seemed. I felt as if there were a pair of eyes at every window. Fortunately, that included my own. Thumps was standing there, gaping like a fool. I waved for him to come out and help, but he stood frozen in place. Then I gave him the "steal-no-matter-what on the next pitch" signal and that finally was enough to get him moving.

"Oh god!" Dancer moaned, leaning back and staring up to the heavens. "I still love him so!" Then he squeezed me so hard I almost fell over. Probably would've in fact, if Thumps hadn't arrived just in time to catch me.

"Go call Buster," I ordered, once I was firmly upright again. Dancer was considerably larger than me and every bit as much a professional athlete. I wasn't making progress towards the apartment with him anymore. "Right now, and tell him I need him here like I've never needed him anywhere before."

"B-but. . ." Thumps stuttered. "B. . . B. . ."

"Do it!" I exploded, angry at last. "Get *something* right, why don't you?"

For just an instant, something died in Thump's eyes. "I. . ." I tried to explain as Dancer squeezed the life out of me and wailed his broken heart out. "I. . ." *I didn't really mean that*, I wanted to say. *I'm just too busy with another crisis to. . .*

It was too late, though. The damage was already done. "Right," Thumps agreed, his eternal smile gone. "I'll go call Buster. That much, I think I can handle."

***

The road trip would've been a total disaster if Pudge hadn't finally found his bat. He went on an absolute tear at the plate, going four for five, two for three, three for four practically every game. He'd begun a beard; the deep-black stubble on his chin combined with the newly-wild look in his eyes made him look like he lived under a bridge and ate small children for breakfast. Soon his biggest problem was that no one would pitch to him. Instead he was intentionally walked, which quite often put him on base behind me.

So what'd I do about it? I encouraged him to steal bases. He'd never be fast, not with his physique. But the first time he made the attempt he got away with it on sheer shock value, and the second on my borrowed smarts. After that the pitchers were almost as paranoid about him as they were about me; it was *humiliating* when a big lumbering dump-truck of a man managed to steal a base off of you. Word got around. This was all to the good; the more paranoia there was in the world the better for us base-stealers. One night, with Buster's permission, Pudge and I toasted our new partnership with half a mug of beer. When Dancer caught back up with us—he was ordered to take three days off and see a counselor—we went absolutely wild. No baseball team can succeed unless all of its parts are working, but on the other hand there's never been a club that doesn't also have deep, fundamental weaknesses built into it. So, it doesn't take much to radically alter the balance of things. Pudge's new success combined with Dancer's drive was enough to upset things sufficiently that we began to climb steadily in the standings. Apparently, our ballet-master had grown a little angry, too. And determined never to be taken advantage of again. We not only won four in a row, but romped our foes by at least a ten-run margin in every single game. The statisticians went nuts trying to keep up.

Our worst weak spot remained Thumps. He was already hitting under his weight, but after the incident in the parking lot he slumped even worse. The coach finally pulled him out of the starting lineup and there were rumors that he was on his way back to AA ball. Pretty soon the only time he was seeing action was when we needed a pinch-runner, or when we'd built up such a lead that the "also-ran" players, who knew that the odds were heavily stacked against their ever seeing the bigs, were on the field. It was a major, humiliating step down for my roommate, one he bore in deep, frigid silence. Thumps grew even colder and quieter after our owner, Mr. Sandrell, came to watch us play in Roswell and addressed the team. "The parent club is taking a beating this year," he explained to us all. "We're going to finish dead last, likely as not. So we've decided that we're going to keep you people, our best prospects, right where you're at. That way, you'll have more time to work with the finest developmental coaching and support staff in the world. I know you all dream of the bigs and that it's hard to wait. But next year there'll be major changes upstairs. And many of you will be moving up." Then he met privately with Pudge and Dancer and I, plus a couple of our best pitchers, and congratulated us on what great years we were having. "Everyone swore you'd screw up," Mr. Sandrell told me last of all. "Everyone in baseball. But you haven't, Cheetah. Not once. In fact, I'm told you're emerging as a team leader. And your numbers are phenomenal." He laughed. "I *knew* you had it in you! Maybe I should talk more players into growing fur. . ." Conspicuously absent from this private reception was Thumps, who at the beginning of the year had been among the four biggest, hottest prospects that were supposed to be the franchise's future. Now, apparently, we were only three.

I'd done many stupid things in my career. Many, many, *many* stupid things. But never had anyone questioned my innate ability to play baseball at the highest professional level. Indeed, my innate talent was why I'd been allowed to screw up so profoundly and for so long. Thumps, however, was apparently not so lucky. He was working as hard as humanly possible, living a clean life, paying strict attention to his coaches, and still getting nowhere. His level of natural ability, it seemed, *was* in question. There *was* doubt as to whether or not he'd make it all the way.

I could only imagine how that must hurt.

By the time we roared into Grenada, home of the league-leading and arch-rival Muskrats, we were hotter than firecrackers on the Fourth of July. The minor-league press, such as it was, converged on Upper Mississippi in droves to watch the expected pyrotechnics. There was thunder and lightning in the air.

Literally, there was thunder and lightning in the air. Hail and tornado warnings, too. Our Friday twi-night double-header was stormed out, then the Saturday game was cancelled because power hadn't yet been restored at the stadium. By Saturday night, therefore, most of us Catfish were feeling pretty restless and full of ourselves. In my own case, it was the first time since spring training that I'd found myself with too much time on my hands. Here it was, eight o'clock on a Saturday night. I was twenty-eight years old, and what was I doing? Lying in a lumpy hotel bed, watching a cartoon channel on the motel's holotank with a sullen, silent roommate. "Thumps," I said finally. "I can't stand it anymore. I'm heading out."

He sort of half-shrugged. "Whatever."

"We aren't subject to bed-checks until midnight," I pointed out, as if he'd argued with me. "It's not like I'm doing anything against the rules."

"Nope," he agreed. Then he half-rolled over onto his side, facing away from me.

"Right," I agreed. "I'll be back by midnight, then. Promise."

He nodded. "See ya."

Most of the time we stayed in cheap motels. They weren't nearly as bad as those in the Dominican Republic, mind you; I wasn't about to complain. But they tended to be of low-enough class that they didn't have bars in the lobbies.

This one, however, did.

I'd promised myself back in my room that I wasn't going to have a drink. I reinforced this intention by swearing mighty oaths as I strode across the lobby. And by the time I eased my way into the little lounge, I'd pretty much convinced myself that all I was going to do was just take a quick look-see and sort of check out the action.

In truth, I was a little nervous about going into the bar. Grenada Mississippi is a rural sort of place and its inhabitants aren't exactly used to dealing with people who claim to be indulging their inner cheetah by growing fur and spots and the like. Sure, I'd run into people on the streets many times before this, mostly while going about my daily business back in Baton Rouge. For the most part they were nice, and even those who weren't tended at least to be tolerant. The worst anyone ever did was ask for an autograph. Somehow, though, bars are different. And this was my first since the big change.

I stepped into the relative darkness, blushing dark red under the fur. . .

. . .and the damnedest thing happened. Which was nothing. Nothing at all. The juke-box played on, the waitresses walked briskly back and forth, and the murmur of conversation went on unchanged.

I smiled, keeping my lips over my fangs, suddenly feeling a lot better. Something in my life, at least, remained just like it had always been. Then I strode the rest of the way in and eased myself up against the bar. "A rum and coke!" I heard myself declare. "Have you got any rum from the Dominican Republic? The stuff'll take the enamel off your teeth, I swear!"

"Sure, hon!" the barmaid trilled, looking me up and down and clearly approving of every spotted inch. "I'll see what I can do."

I looked around the poorly-lit room, seeking team-mates. Pudge Jefferson and Pudge Hiller were sitting together not far away, probably rapt in a discussion about the finer points of catching. Nearer to me sat Dancer with some sort of fruit-filled drink; he was making eyes at a local man who might best be described as pretty. But, other than them, so far as I could tell the coast was clear. I'd just take my drink before anyone noticed, ease back into one of the darker corners. . .

"Why hello, Cheetah!" an acid voice suddenly exploded out of nowhere. "Out for a little drinkie, are we?"

I closed my eyes, sighed, then turned to face Coach Turnbull. "They serve just plain old soda pop here too," I countered. "It isn't my fault if you assumed that..."

"I found you some of that Dominican rum you were asking for, honey!" the barmaid declared, plopping down an oversized glass in front of me. "It's a triple, on the house." She smiled and looked me up and down again. "For helping to improve the scenery, like."

"Damn it!" Turnbull exploded, throwing his hat to the ground and stomping on it. "And damn *you*, Cheetah Jones! Just when I thought you might amaze the bejesus out of me and make good!" His face turned hard and cold. "If you hadn't lied on top of everything else I might've given you another chance. But my marching orders are clear. Go get your personal gear and meet me back here. We're going to get you a separate room, and then in the morning I'll fly you off to wherever you want to go rot for the rest of your life." He shook his head sadly. "God, what a waste of space!"

My mouth fell open. "But... I mean... I was just... It wasn't..."

Suddenly there was a presence at my elbow. "Thanks, Cheetah!" Dancer declared, rubbing up against me in a manner somewhere in the vast unmapped region between very friendly and improper. "I've always wanted to try one of these Dominican rums you go on and on about. I appreciate *so* much your buying this one for me! It was very kind of you."

I tried to engage my tongue, but it wouldn't shift into gear. "Uh..."

"Damn!" Tony muttered, turning bright red. Then he bent over to pick up his hat. "I'm sorry, Cheetah," he said eventually. "It's just that you've done so well and all, and I naturally thought... I mean, I never imagined..." He looked at Dancer, then at me. Finally, he just shook his head and walked away. "Damn!"

"A plain coke for Cheetah, please," Dancer instructed the barmaid. "Charge it to my table." Then he smiled at me again and winked.

"Thank you," I finally said, not referring to the coke.

"You're more than welcome," the left-fielder replied, understanding exactly what I meant. "I owed you one, after all." He smiled. "But even more, you deserved it."

11

Our Sunday game with the Muskrats should've been full of high drama and tension, after all the media buildup and Mother Nature's free spectacle. And I suppose it fulfilled its promise eventually. But for the first two hours or so the most exciting incident was the traditional tee-ball hitting game sponsored by a local bank during the seventh-inning stretch. A six-year-old girl knocked the ball all the way to second base, a feat which won her a brand-new bicycle and free ice cream at a local establishment for her entire family. Other than that, the game was boring as could be. I led off with a single, then stole second and was stranded there. My counterpart, the Muskrat's lead-off hitter, opened with a triple but also was in turn stranded. These remained the offensive highlights of the game right up until the ninth inning. Play was about as routine as routine could get; by the top of the ninth the Muskrat's pitcher had scattered six hits. Our own hurler had allowed five, neither side giving up any runs. So we couldn't claim the pleasure of witnessing a classic pitcher's duel. There weren't even any exciting defensive plays to liven things up. About the only entertainment I found all day, in fact, was glancing over at the Muskrat's bullpen from time to time and grinning.

"Stop that, Cheetah!" Dancer objected at one point, catching me at my little game. "It's not fair to pick on mere children." Then he smiled, showing that he was kidding.

"Heh!" I chuckled back, kicking my feet up on the dugout's front-row bench and relaxing as best I was able in such intense heat and humidity. An old friend had joined the Muskrat's pitching staff during the storm days, it seemed. A nineteen-year-old prodigy of a short-reliever named Reginald Barnes, who was also rather a petulant child. I'd made a fool of him on my first day with the club—Reginald was the kid whose control I'd broken by getting him angry during base-stealing drills. His feelings had been hurt by the resulting demotion to AA ball, it seemed. Instead of rolling with the blow and accepting that the coaching staff knew what was good for him, he'd demanded to be traded. And he'd gotten his wish. "On the count of three," I suggested. Dancer smiled and nodded. "One, two, *three*!" At the last syllable we turned and grinned together, the left-fielder making a silly face as well. It was great fun! By now young Reginald just *had* to be fuming. . .

It was the top of the ninth before the game finally showed signs of breaking free. I led off with a grounder up the middle, the kind of roller that, before I bulked up, would've been an easy out. But now, with just that little extra bit of snap behind it, the ball dribbled through the infield and I was safe at first by a hair. The crowd received my effort with an icy silence, as was to be expected, and while I was dusting myself off I took a moment to think about Herman, whose idea the new muscles had been. I owed him big time, and yet somehow I still hadn't found time to thank him.

The Muskrat pitcher had been on the mound for eight complete innings, working hard in the hot summer sun. I figured that he was probably losing it, getting tired and sloppy. But he held me on first as tightly and professionally as if he were fresh as a daisy. With the game on the line and nobody out old Buster, coaching third, wouldn't give me the steal sign. I couldn't blame him, really. The pitcher and I played footsie back and forth eight or ten times, then he finally served one up to Dancer at the plate. And. . .

. . .*Pow!* My friend hit it long and high and deep, the perfect sacrifice fly. I waited, waited, waited at the bag while the right-fielder positioned himself just-so under the ball and caught it, then tagged-up and ran for second. It wasn't even close: I beat the throw standing up as the crowd began to rumble unpleasantly.

Then it was Donnie Parker's turn at the plate. Parker was another has-been, a player who'd spent most of a season up in the bigs eight years back. But he'd taken a line-drive to the head while there, permanently doubling his vision just enough to drop his batting average a good thirty points. He wasn't a pseudo-coach like old Pudge Jefferson, on the team for the express purpose of sharing his hard-earned wisdom after a distinguished career. Instead, Donnie was a rather pathetic figure who'd once had a bright future but now would never see the bigs again. The true reason he was still playing was that no one had the heart to fire him. Everyone always went out of their way to be nice to Donnie, even our opponents. We understood all too clearly that there but the grace of god went ourselves.

Tragic figure or no, Donnie was a lousy clutch hitter. He fanned, though he managed to run up a full count first. Somewhere along the way the pitcher grew a little distracted, and as a result I slid safely into third.

That brought Pudge Hiller up to bat. Instantly the Muskrat's coach called time and jogged out to the mound, pointing at his right arm on the way. There was going to be a pitching change, about two outs overdue in my opinion, and a right-hander was on his way out to the mound.

Since time was out Buster gestured for me to join him for a private chat in the coach's box. "It's gonna be that spoiled jackass Barnes," he observed, nodding towards the Muskrat bullpen. Then he smiled. "Could it be any more perfect?" I smiled back in the way that best exposed my new fangs, which was exactly what I knew Buster wanted me to do. He slapped me on the back wordlessly, then gently shoved me back towards third base.

There are certain times in baseball when everyone in the stadium is looking at you. Most of those moments happen when you're making plays; during those fleeting seconds a player is far too busy trying not to screw up to worry much about all the eyes staring at him. But there are other times when you *do* have time to think about it, when in fact you can't *not* think about it. Like when you step across the plate after hitting a home run, for example. . .

. . .or when you come walking out of the bullpen for the very first time as part of a new team, with the announcer making a big deal out of the fact so that the home crowd will give you the traditional standing-ovation of a greeting. Most players try to look humble at such moments; they keep their heads down and try to remind themselves that they're as mortal as anyone else. Not Reginald Barnes, however. He *strutted* to the mound with head held high, hat off and general overall bearing as arrogant as if he'd just won his tenth gold medal in the Olympic Games.

"Geez," Buster muttered, loud enough to be heard all the way from the coach's box. "I'm sure glad *that* one's gone."

"Wish you'da kept him," the Muskrat third baseman muttered under his breath. "What a jackass!"

Reginald's delivery was a thing of beauty. During his warmups he pumped fastball after fastball into the catcher's mitt, each of them clocking well over a hundred miles an hour. Then it was time for Pudge to step into the batter's box. He dug in, raised his club of a bat, squinted. . .

. . .and took the first pitch dead in the ribcage.

"Ouch!" the third-baseman muttered in sympathy.

An ugly mutter rumbled through the crowd as Herman came dashing out of the dugout, cold towel and icepack already in hand. A hundred-mile-an-hour fastball is plenty enough to kill a man if it strikes in the wrong place; no one blamed Pudge for moaning and writhing on the ground under Herman's ministrations. After a couple of minutes work, by virtue of a complex feat of applied leverage the diminutive trainer hauled the power-hitter up onto his feet and supported him as he limped first towards the dugout, then the clubhouse, and after that directly to the x-ray machine beyond. Once again the crowd rose to its feet, this time to applaud Pudge for leaving the field under his own power.

The Muskrat *fans*, at least, knew how to show a little class. For it was clear to every knowledgeable eye in the place that Pudge had been beaned, sure as could be. The only thing lacking was definitive proof.

Coach Turnbull sent Thumps out to run for Pudge at first base, then pinch-hit Pudge Jefferson in the number-five slot. The move was logical for several reasons; Jefferson was a lefty, and we needed a new catcher in the game anyway. But most of all, I suspected, Turnbull slid Jefferson into the lineup because of his vast experience and gray hair. *He*, of all people, wasn't going to let a pimply-faced teen rattle him. The umpire went out and had an earnest little discussion with Mr. Barnes, who nodded soberly when it was over. Then the ump settled in behind the plate and called time in. The next pitch was thrown. A strike, on the lower inside corner.

Pudge scowled, stepped out of the batter's box and knocked some dirt out of his spikes, then dug back in. The second pitch arrived. Ball one! Then another. Ball two! Once again Pudge called time and stepped out of the box, fiddling with something near his left knee. Probably a brace of some kind; he wore a ton of them. Meanwhile the Muskrat coach decided that he wanted a conference; the next thing I knew he was jogging out towards the mound again and the whole Muskrat team was converging on him.

Suddenly Buster's lips were at my ear. "Squeeze," he whispered. "It's on."

I gulped. The squeeze play, for my money, was the most exciting, difficult play in baseball. It derived its name from the fact that it was designed to 'squeeze' the defenders, or force them to make difficult decisions much too quickly. Then they'd have to *act* on these same instantaneous decisions as a unit, with total perfection, or else things would go wrong for them in a very large way. On the next pitch, Pudge Jefferson would do his best to get a hit; in any case he'd swing at the pitch, and do everything he could to be obstructive and make a nuisance of himself without quite breaking the rules. If he *did* get a hit, fine and dandy; I'd score easily. And if he didn't. . .

. . .then in that case, I had to *steal* us a run! Meanwhile, Thumps would be tearing up the basepads as well. A single bad throw, a moment's misplaced hesitation and we might just score *twice*.

It was clear from the moment play was resumed that the Muskrats suspected what was up. In fact, that was probably why the mound-conference had been called in the first place; to make sure everyone knew exactly who would cover what once the pressure was on. Barnes went well out of his way to hold me close at third, something that pitchers rarely bothered to do under these conditions. The Muskrats knew what was up, all right. . .

. . .but when I looked over at the first base coach, his hand tapped out the signal regardless. I bared my fangs—either Coach Turnbull didn't think there was much a chance of anyone else on the team getting a hit off of Barnes. . .

. . .or else he had a lot more faith in me than I'd realized. I gulped and made the countersign indicating that I was ready.

Finally, after another flurry of pickoff attempts the long-awaited pitch was delivered to the plate. My heart thundering in my ears, I began driving for home. Old Pudge scowled ferociously, began to swing. . .

. . .then tried and failed to spin away as Barnes's fastball took him in the left thigh.

It was deliberate again, and once more everyone knew it. But this time the Muskrat pitcher was unlucky. Because he was so old and his legs were so beat-up, Pudge Jefferson wore a virtual suit of armor under his uniform from the waist down. The ball struck and bounced off almost as if it had hit a cement wall. . .

. . .and with his eyes narrowed in rage the uninjured Pudge, whose career was already over and who therefore had absolutely nothing left to lose, threw down his bat and charged the mound.

There wasn't anything for it but to join in the fun. After all, I was already sprinting towards the plate at high speed anyway. The Muskrat catcher was rising to his feet and trying to glom onto Pudge's shoulder, to protect his teammate from the hammering that he had to know was richly deserved but which it was his job to prevent regardless. He'd forgotten all about me, apparently. I took his legs out from underneath him quite neatly indeed, shredding flesh all the way with my spikes. Then in an instant I was on my feet, ready for more. . .

. . .until something hard landed on the back of my head, just behind where my left ear was going to end up sometime soon. Then everything went black and stayed that way.

12

I woke up little by little over a period of several hours. The first time I came around, it only lasted for a few seconds. There were faces above me, but they were only swimming blurs. I tried to speak, couldn't, then attempted to reach out and touch them. But before the muscles even got the message I was out again. And so it went on and on and on; each episode of consciousness lasting longer and growing clearer. Eventually I recognized Buster sitting at my bedside, with Dancer alongside him. "Unh!" I grunted intelligently. "Unh-nunh!"

As one they leapt to their feet and stood beside me. "Easy now, son!" Buster warned me, grabbing the hand I tried to raise and lowering it back to my mattress. "You just lie there and take it easy. You're going to be all right, but you've got a subdural hematoma."

"That means you've got a pool of blood in your head, sort of," our left-fielder explained. He was really good at explaining stuff, Dancer was. In another life he might've made a fine teacher. "It's not going to hurt you long-term, but for a little while you're going to have to do exactly what the doctors tell you."

I tried to nod, then realized what a terrible mistake *that* was. Dancer looked at Buster, who nodded. "You've got a hairline fracture in your skull, as well," he explained. "Nothing really serious; the doc had to magnify the x-ray to even see it. But from now on maybe you'd better play with a helmet."

I scowled; helmets were hot, sweaty things. They slowed me down. "Wha. . ." I asked, "Wha. . ."

Buster took over. "The squeeze was on—" he began.

"Sucker beaned Pudge," I interrupted, nodding so slightly that it didn't hardly hurt. "I 'member."

"Both Pudges, actually," Buster continued. "You were at third, coming home." He winced. "Don't get me wrong, Cheetah. I wouldn't have had you do it any other way. But you gave that catcher fifteen stitches and a sprained knee. You should know that. The League's going to be coming to see you about it."

I sort of half-shrugged. Surprisingly, it didn't hurt. "Man's gotta do," I muttered. "Protect my team."

"Right," Buster agreed, nodding. "Like I said, I wouldn't have it any other way. The fact is, I'm gonna be drawing a big suspension myself." He shrugged. Clearly, in his book a man did indeed have to do what a man had to do. "What happened to you was, the third baseman followed you home to help back up the play at the plate. He was running full-out, and I heard from a reporter that he claims he didn't realize that Pudge had been hit by the pitch. When you stood up so suddenly he ran into you from behind. On accident, like. His nose is smeared all over his face."

"Just from hittin' my head?" I asked in wonder.

"No," Buster explained, looking both deeply proud of himself and twenty years younger. "From my fist. He hit *you* with his helmet. Accident my hairy old butt!"

There a long, long silence. "Jeez," I muttered eventually.

"It was *huge*," Dancer continued eventually. "Biggest blow-up in ten years. We'll be talking about it for the rest of our lives. Who was there and who wasn't. Stuff like that." Dancer had a shiner, I realized suddenly. A nasty one. "The whole bench cleared." He smiled. "And Old Pudge decked that jackass pitcher, too. He didn't get back up."

We talked about everything I'd missed for a long, long time, from how poor outnumbered Thumps had taken such a pummeling to how Pudge Hiller actually wasn't all that bad off. "That hillbilly has ribs like barrel-staves," Buster declared proudly. "He'll be playing again in a week."

I was feeling a lot better now, as much from the good company as the medical treatment. "Where's Tony?" I asked at last. "Coach Turnbull, I mean?"

Dancer and Buster looked at each other again and I felt an icy stab in my chest. Was someone else hurt even worse than me? "He's just a couple rooms down," Buster finally explained. "In intensive care."

Pain or no pain, my head rose off my pillow. "What?" I demanded.

"Easy now," Dancer urged, gesturing for me to lay back down. "Remember! This is *serious*! You're *hurt*, Cheetah!"

"Right," I agreed, lying back as ordered. "But. . ."

Buster sighed. "Both benches totally cleared. I mean, it was epic. And that included the coaches. Tony wanted a piece of that pitcher as bad as anyone. But he never made it over the foul line." He shook his head. "You know, I've always wondered what he was doing down in the minors; a dozen organizations would pay top dollar for him with his record. It seems, however, that he's got a bad ticker."

"Old nanites," Dancer explained. "From back in the day. He had heart trouble young and took an experimental treatment. It worked, but because of it he can't take anything more modern to fix his new troubles. He's only got so long, and he knows it."

"So he went back to doing what he truly loved," Buster observed. "Coaching the minors. Who'd have thunk it?"

***

The docs held me for forty-eight hours of observation at first, then extended it to seventy-two when my brainwaves kept on doing funny stuff. "You expect *my* brain to be normal?" I demanded of my doc. But it didn't do any good; I was stuck. When the rest of the team headed back to Baton Rouge for the next game I didn't have any more visitors, either.

You can only watch a cartoon channel just so long. . .

I wasn't actually hooked up to anything anymore except for some monitors on my head that would work just fine anywhere on the hospital grounds. So, in exchange for a solemn promise not to try and get up and walk around, they gave me a little power-chair and let me zip around to the conservatory and the chapel and such. The staff seemed very proud of their conservatory and maybe they had a right to be. But I wouldn't know; I never made it there.

Tony was out of intensive care by the time I got my new wheels, and his new room wasn't far. I spent pretty much all of my three days under observation sitting with him, except for when the League came to hear me swear on my mightiest oath that, just like the third baseman who'd run into me, I'd not realized that Pudge had been hit by the pitch. Apparently, I explained, both of us must've been at an especially bad angle to see that part. I blamed the spiking thing on the fact that the catcher wasn't blocking the plate in a defensive crouch, the way that he should've been and the way that we always practiced. "It wasn't my fault," I summed up, picturing Buster laughing his butt off as I employed my favorite phrase from the bad old days. And Tony *did* laugh when I told him what I'd done, so hard that his beepers beeped and his flashers flashed and a nurse came running in.

"Get this, Cheetah," he chortled as the nurse reset all the alarms. "You ain't gonna believe it. But I actually convinced my investigator that I was on my way out to *stop Pudge*!" Then we laughed again and the alarms needed attention a second time. But the nurse didn't seem to mind.

Eventually, we ran out of things to laugh about and silence set in. "I guess you heard about my heart?"

I nodded silently. "Coach, you don't hafta. . ."

He raised a hand in protest. "No, son. It's all right. Here, we're just two gimps together in the hospital." Then he sighed. "It's all true," he admitted. "There's about a hundred of us who took the early meds while they were still experimental—not that we had much of a choice! But it immunized us to the newer nanites, so we can't get anything more advanced done. There's not enough of us, you see, to justify the research it'd take to work something out. Not while there's about a bajillion others waiting for the same researchers to fix *their* problems." He scowled slightly. "They say this was just a preview, not the main show. I'll be out of here in a week, then I'll pretty much be fine again right up until the Big Day. They say there's always hope, so long as you're sucking air. But. . ."

There was another long, long silence. I've heard that nobody else ever knows what to say to a dying man either. So I suppose it was all right.

"Anyway," the coach continued, scowling. "I'm really glad it wasn't blackout time. Because, well. . ." He sighed. "I'm *so* sorry that I got you wrong about that drink-thing. I mean—you and Dancer, and. . ."

I couldn't help it. I started laughing again, so hard that I was afraid a nurse would show up to reset *me*. "Don't sweat it," I finally sputtered. "In fact. . ."

Tony leaned forward, baffled.

You're out of your mind, a little voice whispered in my left ear. *You got away clean; you don't have to own up to this! No one will ever know.* "Look," I finally said. "I don't even know why I'm telling you this, but somehow I need to. I admit it; the drink was mine. Dancer covered me out of friendship and team loyalty. Dominican rum is about the *last* thing he'd ever drink."

Tony's face hardened for a second, then he let his head fall back onto his pillow. "I see," he said eventually.

I sighed and looked out the window. "So, I'm guilty. I got bored, and I messed up."

There was another long silence. "Well," he said at last. "Then it's a good thing that we're just two gimps here together in a hospital ward then. Because otherwise I might have to fire your butt. And, Cheetah, if you don't realize it yet, that would just about break whatever little heart I might have left."

13

They wouldn't let me play or even work out much for another week, once I caught back up with the team. Buster, who was filling in for Tony, kept me extra-busy nonetheless. My guess was that word had come down to him from on high that I wasn't to be allowed to grow bored. Imagine that!

Anyway, he assigned me not one but two full-time jobs. "First," he said, "you're behind on your shrink-sessions. Not because you've done anything wrong, I know. But they still need to be made up. We've got a schedule all worked out for you."

I gritted my teeth and nodded.

"Second," he said, raising his eyes to meet mine, "I've got a special request."

My eyebrows rose. I looked really good doing that, I knew, as a cheetah. Where before, I'd just looked vacantly stupid.

"Thumps," he said. "Fix him."

My brows rose further. "Isn't that, like, *your* job?"

Buster's gaze fell to the floor. "It is," he acknowledged. "And I've failed at it. We're going to rehab him from the fight injuries here in Baton Rouge, since we can carry him on the disabled list and it won't hurt us any. Then we're going to give him an at-bat or two to rebuild his confidence after what happened, to show that him getting beat up so bad hasn't got anything to do with anything." He gulped. "Then we're going to demote him to AA level ball. Between you and I, I doubt he'll ever be back."

I nodded sadly. "He hasn't got the head for the bigs."

"It's not his head!" Buster snarled. "It's his testicles! At the plate he's afraid to swing, on-base he's afraid to steal. . ." He sighed. "Did you know that he's a track star? Never played ball at all in high school. The previous owners thought anyone that fast could be trained to hit, field, and throw. And he *can* do all of those things, now. But what's he's not is *tough*! Apparently track stars don't have to make complex decisions under pressure or know when it's time to charge the mound and face the music later." He sighed. "You. . . If anything you've got too much in the way of testicles. You're not afraid of nothin'. It's like night and day." He shook his head. "I know you're no coach, Cheetah. And you're surely not being paid to be one. A few months back, I couldn't even imagine asking you to do this. But, do you think that maybe you can help this kid find his manhood?"

Buster's request weirded me out. So did my counseling session that afternoon. It was really strange; for once, I *wanted* to talk about something. "Are you *sure* that this fur coat can't change who I am inside?" was the first thing I asked Dr. Forster, once I was all settled in and he'd asked me about the knot on my head and all that polite stuff.

He blinked, twice. "That's the same thing you asked me last time we talked," he pointed out, crossing his legs. "Are you certain that something isn't bothering you?"

I frowned, then shook my head. "Well. . . It's strange, doc. Hard to explain, kind of."

He smiled slightly. "You're improving. Feeling better about yourself. Aren't you? You haven't messed up, like you invariably used to do. And you can't figure out why."

It was my turn to blink. "I haven't messed up *yet*, more like," I countered. "Though I tried once just last week, when I got bored. Even then though, it sort of. . ." I shrugged, at a loss for words. "It was halfhearted, like. I was being stupid on purpose, just *asking* to get caught. I mean, if I'd really wanted to get away with a quick drink there were a million smarter ways. . ." I sighed. "I felt kinda bad inside about it even while it was going down." I wriggled in my chair. "Like I was about to hurt myself, but part of me didn't want that anymore."

Slowly, the doctor tilted his head to one side, considering. "So," he said eventually. "You used to need to hurt yourself. But now you're not who you used to be, and therefore you don't need to cause yourself pain. Is that a fair summation?"

I wasn't quite certain what a 'summation' was, but it seemed to reflect the general idea. "Yeah. I guess."

Slowly, the doctor smiled. Then, still smiling, he removed his glasses and polished the lenses. "There's a lot of factors at work here," he explained slowly. "One is of course that you *are* going through a lot of big changes physically, in who and what you are. Who you see in the mirror every morning, even in your grooming and personal habits. There are quite a few men and women in this business who believe that there just might be significant therapeutic value to major makeovers like the one you're having, because it forces a change in self-image at a very deep level. It gives those who *need* to change, in other words, a sort of excuse or maybe even self-permission to grow and develop in new directions. With physical change can come psychological change." He put his glasses back on. "I'm beginning to suspect that just maybe there's something to that theory."

I nodded.

"But in this case there's clearly a lot more at work than just that." He scowled. "At this point, I have to change the subject a little. While I currently specialize in dealing with physical transformation cases like your own, for years before that I was a general therapist treating all sorts of patients. I'm a fully qualified psychiatrist, Cheetah. And while I was engaged specifically to do transformation counseling with you, as is invariably the case other issues have arisen." His scowl intensified. "I've been torn between trying to help you deal with your *real* problems and sticking strictly to the job I've been engaged to do. The job that you've given me *permission* to do." He sighed. "Of all the cases I've ever dealt with, in this one regard yours has been the most difficult. I've tried to help you a little around the edges, in ways that you probably haven't noticed. I took the Hippocratic Oath, after all. Yet, at the same time you unquestionably have the right to demand that we remain strictly on topic." He shrugged his shoulders. "So, before this discussion can proceed any further, I need to know something. Am I just your shrink regarding the cheetah fur, or am I your therapist overall? It's something that needs to be clarified."

I looked down at the floor. He had a point, I guessed, but. . .

"I'll also add," Dr. Forster continued, "that if I'm your therapist overall, I'm going to lead you down some painful paths. To places you don't want to go. Because I think that you very, *very* badly need to go there."

I continued to stare at the floor. "You think this is what's helping me then? The therapy?"

"Among other things," the doc replied. "You're also living in a highly supportive environment as well, which is of incalculable value. Almost an ideal one, even. But. . . a lot of that support is coming from the fact that you're making friends and earning the respect and trust of others. You've never managed that trick before, have you?"

I gulped, then spoke the truth. "No."

"You're venting your anger here with me, instead of on the world in general. And, more importantly perhaps, on yourself." He shook his head. "Heaven knows you've got plenty to be angry about! It's no crime for someone with your past to be enraged to the very core."

I gulped. "You mean. . . I'm not just being a wimp, being mad about my mom? And. . . And. . ."

The doctor's face softened. "No, Cheetah, you're not. You've risen out of hell, son! Sheer unadulterated hell! Is it any wonder that you still carry a few hot embers and personal demons with you?"

Suddenly everything went blurry. "You don't know. . . I mean, I haven't told you. . ."

Then the doctor was by my side, hugging me and offering tissues. "I know you haven't," he said softly. "And that's okay. Whenever you're ready, and not until then." He smiled again. "We've got all the time in the world."

***

Being under orders not to work out left me plenty of opportunities to think about stuff. I'd grown up in hell, the doc had told me, and god knew he was right enough about that. But still carrying demons? Well. . . What *was* that little voice in my head that urged me to get drunk and buy underaged hookers and get awful tattoos, I asked myself, if not a sort of demon? So I went by the clinic and signed some papers making Doc Forster my overall, general-purpose shrink. The front office said nothing about it, for which I was grateful.

Even though I couldn't practice I still hung around the team as much as I could. They'd settled in for a long homestand, and despite the fact that half the lineup was either on the disabled list or suspended from the big fight we were still playing .500 ball. This wouldn't have been so great, but the Muskrats had gone into an awful tailspin. Not only had they suffered as many casualties as we had, but their own man was ultimately in the wrong and they knew it. Baseball was a cold-blooded game in some respects; I didn't bear the Muskrat third-baseman a grudge for defending his catcher any more than I figured their catcher hated me for defending Pudge. But the chain has to eventually come to an end somewhere, and once violence has broken out feelings can become intense. People don't *like* having to defend someone who's clearly in the wrong, even if they can't admit it right out. In fact, it upsets them at a very deep and profound level. So they take it out in other ways. I could easily imagine the fights and arguments that must be erupting all over the Muskrat clubhouse, as people took sides and assigned blame and pointed fingers. No one could play effective ball under such conditions. It was a miracle they ever won a game at all.

It was mid-August, and for the first time we were catching a whiff of the pennant.

Thumps was on the disabled list too; at his first step towards the mound during the big dustup the much-larger Muskrat first baseman tackled him. Then he and the right-fielder and second-baseman had proceeded to spend the next several minutes pounding him into the grass. The bad news was that he'd lost a tooth and was seriously bruised almost all over. The good news was that nothing worse than that was wrong with him and the League investigators had decided that a single step towards the mound, under the circumstances, wasn't enough justification to penalize a man. So he was one of the few of us to walk away scot-free. If you didn't count the dental work, that was.

I walked away clean, too, as did the Muskrat who broke my head. The League accepted our story about how we thought the ball was still in play. The catcher was awarded a two-week suspension and a large fine, and both Pudge Jefferson and Reginald Barnes drew thirty days and a stiffer fine still. Pudge laughed when the official letter arrived. As an ex-big-league star, he could easily afford even the most punishing minor-league level financial penalty. "As for the suspension, I'll appeal and then appeal again," he explained. "That'll take at least until November. Long after the season's over, in other words. When I'll be retired anyway. Anyone else wanna try and bean my butt before the end of the year?"

Buster, as a coach who at least in theory was supposed to be nurturing the players instead of smearing their noses all over their faces, drew ninety days and enough of a fine to actually sting a little. He too laughed, then proudly framed the official reprimand and hung it on his office wall next to his ancient Golden Glove. He appealed too, but "Just so I have time to set up a base-stealing clinic to be held off league property, so those three months aren't totally wasted." You had to love Buster. You just *had* to.

But Thumps and I walked away clean, or limped away, or staggered away, or whatever. We watched the games in street clothes from the dugout, sometimes sitting together and sometimes not, and then spent the rest of the day in our shared apartment, where Thump's mother had practically moved in to wet-nurse him back to health. "I'll get it!" she kept saying whenever her son rose to do anything, and I never ate so much cannelloni in my life. No matter how Thumps protested she was always at his elbow, adjusting, primping, fluffing. "My baby's been *hurt!*" she'd declare whenever he tried to do anything for himself. "You know, Mr. Simpson's still hiring down at the factory. People don't beat each other up there when they can't get along. . ."

I stayed in my bedroom, mostly, and thought. Thumps was on his way to a factory job, all right. Anyone could read the tea-leaves. And, after coming so close to the dream, such ordinariness would be even more soul-killing than usual. It hadn't been at all fair of Buster to ask me to get involved in the kid's problems, to try and turn him around. Not only were turnarounds not exactly my specialty, but none of this was in any way at all my fault, now was it?

But my fault or no, Buster expected results. And I couldn't let *him* down. So, one day when the team didn't play and I had nothing to at all to do except sit and eat cannelloni, I thought back over every minute of my relationship with Thumps. I also considered what Buster had said about him lacking the machismo for the game and decided he was right. Next I pondered what he said about me maybe having a surplus of manhood, and then about Thump's mother, and then about *my* mother and, well. . . I grew very angry indeed for a time. But it was all worth it. Because when I was done being angry I worked out the kind of half-crazy gonzo plan that only someone gifted with a little too much testosterone and not nearly enough brain tissue could ever come up with.

A plan that, I reckoned, just might do the trick.

A couple days later Thumps and I found ourselves zooming up I-55 on my scooter, running ten over the posted limit and living every mile to the hilt. Thumps had always been jealous of my scooter. He'd confided to me once that he'd always wanted a motorbike of his own but his mother had made him promise he'd never buy one because it was too dangerous. So it hadn't been any great trick to persuade him to come along and help me with a 'little errand' up in Mississippi. "It's no big deal," I explained to him. "But I just had this head injury, see? I don't want to be alone in case I get woozy and have to pull over. . ."

And so far things were going well indeed. I whistled a happy little tune to myself as I swung out into the passing lane and overtook first an RV, then a line of heavy trucks. Thump probably felt like a very brave and bad boy indeed under his brand-new full-face helmet and reflective visor. He'd lied to his mother about where he was going, after all, and riding was always an adventure in and of itself.

It was well after dark when we arrived in Grenada. I was a little tight and stiff from the ride and Thumps was probably suffering even worse, not being used to a bike's hard seat. Still, he seemed perfectly happy as I cruised up and down the peaceful residential streets.

"Whatcha lookin' for, Cheetah?" he finally asked, leaning forward and shouting so I could hear him. "Is something wrong?"

"No," I replied as at long last I found what I sought. A scooter very much like my own, of a slightly different model but of the same exact color, was sitting a nice dark shadow where a large tree was shading it from the streetlight. I smiled, killed the motor, and coasted to a stop just behind it. "Everything's going just fine."

"Wow!" Thumps declared as he dismounted. "This is so much fun! I mean, I never. . ." Suddenly, he realized that I was pulling a large screwdriver out from under my seat. "Uh. . . Cheetah?"

"Yes, Thumps?" I replied in a patient tone as I began removing the parked scooter's license plate. "What is it?"

"I. . . Uh. . ." he protested, looking around nervously.

"It's all right," I assured him. "We're just borrowing it. I've done this before, lots of times." Though, I didn't tell him, in the past I hadn't bothered sliding a pair of hundred-dollar bills into the glovebox to compensate my fellow rider for his troubles. Soon I had the 'borrowed' plate mounted securely on my own bike. "Come on. Everything's going to be just fine."

"I. . . Uh. . ." Thumps stuttered. This was the crucial moment, the point at which my team-mate was most likely to back out on me. But by my figuring it probably took even more in the way of testosterone to stand up to one's trusted friend and deliberately strand one's self on foot in a strange town in the middle of the night as it did to just smile and pretend that everything was indeed still perfectly fine. Which was what Thumps, bless his innocent soul, finally did.

"A-a-all right," he finally said dubiously, climbing up onto the pillion behind me. "I g-g-guess—"

I never did find out what Thumps guessed, because instead of listening to him I fired up the bike, gunned it, and thereby drowned out his voice in the wind and the roar of the motor. I knew exactly where I was, having studied up a little on Grenada geography ahead of time, and so was able to drive us directly to the Grenada Municipal Sports Complex and Stadium. . .

. . .Home of the Mighty Muskrats AAA Baseball Team!

"Uh," Thumps protested as I cruised by at low speed, checking out the setup. There were security cameras, I noted, but placed in such a way that I didn't think they could cover anything right up against the building. "Uh. . ."

"Everything's *fine*," I reassured my nervous friend. "In fact, they couldn't be more perfect. Just keep your helmet on and your visor down, and I'll have to make sure that my tail stays in my pants leg as well. If we do that, what can possibly go wrong?"

The clubhouse was located behind the stadium; another slow circuit of the neighborhood confirmed my memory of the setup. There wasn't a soul around; the Muskrats had left two days before on a road trip to Arkansas. Even better, the whole area around the back of the place looked like an overgrown park; Mississippians loved their magnolia trees, and there were *huge* ones all around the building.

"Whew!" I heard Thumps sigh as I gave the scoot a little gas and effortlessly whirred us away. But his relief didn't last long. Within seconds I had us parked on a residential street just opposite the clubhouse.

"Cheetah," Thumps objected again. "I don't know what—"

"There's a little window in the visitor's locker room," I interrupted him. "It was always open, remember? To clear the stink." I grinned and showed my fangs, though Thumps couldn't possibly see them through the reflective visor. "It was even kept open during the big storms. I bet it's still up now."

For the first time, my friend began to see the possibilities. "I could get through that," he said after a time. "Or at least I think I could. And maybe you, too!"

"Both of us, for sure!" I countered.

"But. . ." Thumps stuttered again. "But. . ."

"Come on!" I declared, grabbing my carefully-prepared bag of goodies from under the seat. "Let's go!"

No alarms sounded as Thumps and I dashed through the big magnolia trees and crushed ourselves tight up against the building. This didn't surprise me any, as my boyhood experiences with breaking and entering had taught me much about the limitations of motion-detectors vis-à-vis large trees that sway in the wind. The cameras probably got a shot of us, but in plain black riding gear and visored-helmets we might've been anyone.

The little window *was* open, just as predicted—even out here in the fresh air it was easy to detect a trace of locker-room funk. "You first," I directed Thumps, cupping my hands so as to offer him a leg-up.

"I. . . Uh. . ." he stuttered again. "I mean, Cheetah. . ."

"Suit yourself," I answered, shrugging theatrically and looking around for inspiration. There was a medium-sized trash dumpster just a few feet away from where I needed it; without hesitating I strode over and put my shoulder to it. *SCREE!* the long-rusted wheels complained. *SCREEE-EEE-EEE!*

"Jesus Christ!" Thumps complained, bouncing up and down like he was terrified or something. "Stop that!"

The dumpster was still a long way from being in place. *SCREEEEE!*

"Damn it!" Thumps finally protested. Then, seemingly without effort, he leapt up, grabbed onto the windowsill and pulled himself up inside. "Here!" he declared, reaching down to offer me a hand. "Just stop that racket!"

I blinked. There was no way on earth that *I'd* ever have been able to leap so high from a standing start. And he was faster than me, on top of that! What exactly was I unleashing on the unsuspecting world of professional baseball, anyway? But it was *far* too late to change my mind now. So instead of arguing I accepted the offered hand and sort of clambered in after him.

The locker room was dark and empty, which was all to the good. "I don't remember there being any motion-sensors in here," I explained into the silence. "Which makes sense, considering they use robo-janitors. But if the lights come on or if you notice *anything* weird, run for the bike. There's not a cop in the state who can catch either of us."

"Right," Thumps agreed, panting lightly. He sounded steadier, now that he was fully committed. "You've got lights, I presume?"

"Yeah," I agreed, pulling a pair of tiny penlights from the pouch and turning them on. "We have three things we need to do, as I see it."

"Three?" Thumps asked. "Then let's get them done and get out of here! Jeez, if Mom ever finds out. . ."

"She won't," I reassured him. "Just think about those bruises you're still wearing under that riding jacket."

Thumps scowled and nodded. "And your fractured skull. And Pudge's ribs. I get it, all right. And, well. . . Let's do this!"

"Good!" I answered, smiling again. "So, here's what we're after. . ."

By the time I was done explaining Thumps was laughing so hard that it took him twice as long to execute his mission as it should've. So I took a little extra time with my home-made template and brown spray can, painting primitive Baton Rouge Catfish logos on the Muskrat's lockers and then epoxy-ing all the doors shut. In fact, I ended up with so much extra time on my hands that I thought of a little something extra. I was still standing on the locker-room bench urinating into the air-vents of the locker belonging to a certain Reginald Barnes when Thumps finally arrived, carrying our main prize. "All right!" he declared, as excited as a ten-year-old on Christmas morning. "I've got it!"

"Good," I replied, finishing up my self-appointed task. "Care to take a squirt?"

Thumps's face screwed up in revulsion. "No. In fact, I think. . . No!"

I smiled again. "You come from a higher-class neighborhood than I do," I explained. "You lucky kid. Now come on! Let's get out of here!"

***

I'd done a pretty fair job planning out our little raid, even if I did say so myself. But I *did* make one tiny slipup, which didn't become evident until Thumps and I were again standing beside my scooter, eager to mount up and make miles.

"What do you mean, it won't fit?" Thumps demanded.

"Scooters don't have a lot of room in them," I explained, shrugging. "And that damn muskrat suit is a *lot* bulkier than I expected." I frowned. "Maybe we oughta just go back and throw it in the dumpster. . ."

"Forget *that*!" Thumps replied, "Not after coming all this way!"

And so it came to pass that Thumps rode all the way back home to Baton Rouge on the back of my scooter dressed as The Mighty Muskrat. Even the head fit just fine over his helmet, without ripping it too badly. Being the discreet sort I took backroads most of the way home, and because it was so late we didn't meet much traffic. But whenever we did Thumps waved and capered and generally messed around so enthusiastically that he nearly wrecked us twice. We were pretty exhausted when we got back to the apartment. The suit fit just fine in the little storage area under our stairs, though Thumps seemed a little disappointed to take it off. We had time for what amounted to a long nap before reporting back to the stadium. When we got there my roomie was still sort of sparkling, full of laughter and life in precisely the way that'd been missing for so long. Buster noticed right away.

"Cheetah?" he asked me, looking across the locker room to where Thumps was engaging in his first towel-fight in heaven only knew how long. "What. . . I mean. . ."

"Get him to the plate just as soon as you possibly can," I said. "Don't wait a minute longer than you can help. The rest you don't want to know about. Really and truly, you don't."

So it was that Thumps suited up a few days earlier than he really should've, pinch-hit in the bottom of the eighth. . .

. . .and drove in the game-winning run.

Soon I was back in the lineup as well, and for the first time our team began to play the way it'd always been meant to. Thumps got two more solid hits off the bench, then he found himself back in the lineup. He was taking risks now, committing himself, being more assertive and self-confident both at the plate and on the basepads. I even cut back a little on the base-stealing, he was hitting so well. . .

. . .and at long, long last, our team was firing on all cylinders. Even better, no one was whispering about Thumps slipping down a league anymore. "You said I don't want to know," Buster said to me one day while we were watching Thumps do his wind-sprints. "And knowing you like I do, I don't doubt your word for a second. But I want you to know that whatever it was that you did, you made me proud."

"Aw," I said, looking down at my shoes. "It wasn't no big thing. My great pleasure, in fact. And besides. . . I owed him for the cannelloni, you see."

14

By Labor Day weekend we were playing to sellout crowds. That almost never happens in the minors; usually the clubs are forced to scrabble and struggle and offer a thousand promotional gimmicks just to fill the stands a quarter full. People simply aren't as interested in minor-league pennant races as they are the ones in the bigs. Partly that's because even AAA baseball is by virtue of it own title admitting to the world that it's second-rate, and partly because as soon as a player achieves something resembling stardom he's immediately plucked from the fold and taken to join the parent organization. But our talent wasn't being plucked; Mr. Sandrell had made it clear that he wanted us to stay right where we were for the rest of the year and keep working with the coaches who were doing us so much good. Plus, the big fight with the Muskrats had fired up the fanbase to an unusual degree— why, there were even rumors floating around that rabid Catfish fans had desecrated the Muskrat clubhouse and stolen their mascot in revenge! Can you *imagine* such a thing?

And, well. . .

About half the fans these days showed up wearing cheetah-spots in one form or another.

"It makes me nervous sometimes," I explained to my shrink on Labor Day Friday. "I mean, all those people. . . if they knew the real me, they wouldn't wear that stuff. Instead, they'd demand I be locked up."

"Why do you think that?" he asked.

I sighed. "I'm. . . I mean, I've always been. . ." There was a long, long silence.

"But now you can't even say it anymore, can you? That you're a screwup, I mean?"

I tried to speak, did my level best to prove him wrong. But somehow I couldn't.

He smiled. "You've climbed far and fast, Cheetah. In the really important ways you've climbed higher than ever before in your life. It's natural that when you look down you should see a growing abyss and be afraid of falling back into it." His smile faded. "But you're *not* going to fall, are you? Because now *you're* in control of what you do and who you are. Not some blind, enraged demon from your past."

I nodded slowly. "But I. . . I mean. . . I still haven't told you. . ."

The doctor smiled again. "I'm still ready whenever you are. There's no rush at all."

We went on to sweep all five games that weekend, while sputtering Grenada went two and two. Now we were only one game back with five left to play.

The last one would be against the Muskrats, at home in Baton Rouge. Even in the big-league cities, knowledgeable sports fans took note and made plans to be near a television that night.

Anything might happen.

***

That last week was a busy one for us all. And it *was* of course the last week of the season; over the years the minor leagues have tried from time to time to generate enough enthusiasm to support playoffs and a minor league championship series, but the fans never quite cough up enough bucks to keep things going. So the end of the regular season marked the end of the line for us Catfish, and the division title was the highest laurel to which we could reasonably aspire.

But we wanted it. Bad!

This state of affairs was a bit odd as well. The sad fact is, minor-league players usually have as much trouble taking themselves seriously as their fans do. All most of us ever think about are the bigs, bigs, bigs. If we're rounding third and see that the outfielder's about to make his throw, a minor-leaguer will tend to hold-up where a major-leaguer might dig in and give it his all, on the grounds that a pointless victory isn't worth risking a possible career-ending injury over. The longer a player is in the minors, the more risk-averse he becomes. The fans know it, the players know it, the coaches know it. . . The only people blissfully unaware of the true state of things are the promotional types, who spend their days in the front office trying to sell "future stars" and "traditional hard-nosed baseball" to the jaded public. Most minor-league seasons end more with a whimper than a roar.

But not this one! I'd only spent part of one season in the bigs, and we'd finished in fourth. The divisional race had been unusually close that year, however, and we weren't statistically eliminated until three days before the end of the season. So I'd very much been in a big-league pennant race, had felt the pressures and been right in the center of it all. Yet I hadn't detected half as much raw need, half the desire to win and dominate and be the top dog among my teammates that I felt every single hour radiating from my fellow Catfish. It was like night and day, something I'd never seen before. In fact, I'd never even *imagined* such total focus.

Maybe if the locker room in my big league team's clubhouse had felt more like *this* one, I might already be wearing a championship ring?

"All *right!*" Dancer declared, clenched fists raised above his head in the universal human gesture for victory. "All *right!*"

I reached over and high-fived my friend. I'd scored in the bottom of the ninth, and so was already sitting in the dugout when Pudge Hiller hit it out of the park and drove both Dancer and Thumps home for a 6-4 win. "All right!" I agreed. Nothing more needed to be said—the truly important aspects of our communications weren't taking place at the verbal level. Instead we just looked at each other and smiled. The crowd was still going nuts outside.

"And Grenada's just lost!" Coach Turnbull declared, following Dancer down the little flight of stairs that we always swore someone was going to fall down someday. "It's official. We're tied!"

"Hooray!" everyone declared, breaking out in cheers. Naked and seminaked men danced about and hugged each other in joy. I'd never seen anything like it. Then the pandemonium finally eased off a little.

"All right, guys," Tony continued, once he had everyone's attention again. "None of us here are stupid. It all comes down to tomorrow. So let's go home, get a good night's rest and come back tomorrow fresh and rested, just like we always do. . ." He grinned. ". . .ready to kick some serious Muskrat butt!"

"Yay!" everyone cheered. Soon we were dancing up and down the aisles again. I was a little surprised when Tony eased up next to me and tapped me on the shoulder—it was so loud that he had to press his mouth up against my ear to make himself heard. ". . .in my front office," I finally made out. "Soon as you're cleaned up."

My eyebrows rose, and Tony nodded, letting me know that I'd heard right. "All right!" I confirmed at the top of my lungs. "I'll be there!"

He smiled, then leaned close to my ear again. "Take your time!" he shouted, gesturing at all the merriment. "You earned this, as much as any of them. Maybe even more!"

***

I was still thinking about my visit with Coach Turnbull in his office the next morning, while sitting in my shrink's chair. "So, this Raymond kid really means a lot to you?" Dr. Forster asked me from the other side of his big, heavy desk.

"Yeah," I agreed after the slightest pause. "I guess he does, even though we've only met twice. I'm not sure why." I sighed and shook my head. "It wasn't until last night that Tony told me he was coming to the game after all. Up until then it looked like he'd be too sick."

"But you did already know that the season-closer was going to be a benefit game for the Cancer Society," he pointed out.

"Oh, yes!" I agreed. "Tony and I both signed the special letter inviting him to come sit in the dugout." I sighed again. "But. . . That was before this turned into such a big game. And now. . ."

"Ah," the doctor agreed, seeming to understand at last. "You're nervous."

"I don't want to look bad in front of him," I explained. "I don't want him to have a bad day. I mean. . ." I shuffled my feet, then looked down at the tabletop. "It really bothers me, that he might not have fun."

"He doesn't have much time left, does he?"

"No," I answered, my voice soft and low. "He doesn't. And what little he has. . . He wants to spend part of it with us. With me."

"He's young, he's helpless, he's innocent, he's suffering, he looks up to you, and he doesn't have much time left," the doctor observed. "That's enough to get to anyone, Cheetah."

There was a long, long silence. My eyes teared up. Then I took a deep, ragged breath. "He reminds me of my kid brother," I said finally. "After."

My shrink's left eyebrow rose. "After?"

I nodded. "After." Then I shook my head and sighed. "Remember how I told you about how things were when I grew up? About how Mom always had her boyfriends over?"

"Yes. Of course."

"Well. . . They weren't exactly 'boyfriends', Doc. Though she called 'em that. Or at least most of 'em weren't boyfriends. She was a hooker; that's how she paid for her weed and pills. I never knew who my daddy was and I never will. My little brother? He probably had another daddy still."

Doctor Forester's face remained impassive. "I see."

I sighed. . . "And sometimes. . ." My face screwed up, but I forced myself to go on. "Sometimes, Doc, when the money was short she sold more than just herself. At first, when I was really little, it didn't mean nothin' to me where I put my mouth. But when I got older and figgered it out better, well. . . I told you that I was strong and fast. By the time I turned twelve there wasn't too many men willing to try and take what I wasn't about to willingly give."

"I'm sorry," he said eventually.

"Heh!" I snorted, the sound wet and bubbly. "You think *you're* sorry! All the other kids knew what Mom was, and her johns talked." I looked down at the desk again. "So I didn't have any secrets. And I found out that a hard fist shut down a laughing mouth pretty quick. So I didn't have any friends. Just kids I knew were laughing behind my back."

Forster's eyes blinked, slowly.

"Anyway," I said, after staring off into space for a long, long moment, "Like I said, I got to be pretty hard to sell. But Mom, she was a lucky whore. Because by then Duncan was just about old enough. He was six years younger than me, Duncan was. And he worshipped me like a god. He wanted to go where I went, play when I played, eat what I ate." I sighed again. "I raised him, I suppose, in that he got raised at all." My fists balled. "Mom always made sure I had him back home by evening, in case she needed him."

"You didn't have anyone else?" my therapist asked. "Nowhere to go?"

"Heh!" I replied. "Half the kids I knew, their moms were whores too! I had grandma, sure enough, but she lived in Topeka and *never* came to visit. Her and Mom, they hated each other." I smiled sadly. "It's not like anyone really cared much about people like us."

Forster nodded, but said nothing.

"So… The more I watched this go on, the madder I got. Finally I had a real brainwave. There was this little place up in the attic, where no adult could get to. Too small and tight, see? It was cold up there in the winter, and hotter than hell in the summer. But it was a *safe* place. Or so I figured it. 'Go up there every night after I bring you home!' I told my brother. 'Go up there and them nasty men can't do you wrong no more'."

"Actually," the therapist observed, "it sounds like a remarkably good plan, considering how young you were and what you were dealing with. All by yourself, mind you, and without support."

I scowled. "It was world-class stupid! The next john that wanted him paid Mom, then looked all over for him. She wouldn't give the money back, so he beat the crap out of her until she ran away." I looked down at the table again. "When he beat Mom, she screamed, and that got little Duncan all scared. So he started crying, and..." My voice trailed away to nothing.

"And?" the doc asked.

"Sucker went ape! The dude was drunk and high on I don't know how many kinds of crap. He tried to get Duncan to come out, but he wouldn't. So he set the attic on fire, to *drive* him out."

"Damn!" Forster whispered.

"Heh!" I snorted. "Just about then I got home, and what greets me in the hallway? A hopped-up monster with a lighter in his hand, lots of smoke, and the smell of my little brother *cooking* as he screamed." I raised my eyes and tried to meet those of Forster, but he had to look away. Then I lowered them again, so that a good and decent man wouldn't have to deal with what I knew was to be found there. "He was all the way squeezed into the back like I'd told him to do, and his only way out was already burning. So I got a big stewpot, filled it with water, and poured on the fire. Three times did the trick; after that there was enough space for me to wriggle back and drag Duncan out. But..." I scowled again. "Three times, I said! Keep in mind, that included running through the house, filling up the pot at the sink, climbing back up the steps with that big, heavy thing... He got burned all to hell."

"What about the son... what about the man who set the fire?" Forster demanded. "Did he help you?"

I looked up again and smiled. It wasn't pretty, I was sure. "He tried to stop me. Said Duncan'd either come out and give him what was coming to him or he could damn well roast."

"Oh," Forster replied, beginning to understand. His face sort of melted. "Cheetah... I mean..."

"He burned up in the fire," I explained truthfully, if a bit incompletely. "I smelled him cook just like I smelled Duncan cook. And don't expect me *ever* to feel too damn bad about that!"

"You were thirteen," he whispered. "Jesus!"

"Almost thirteen," I replied, shrugging. "Anyway... The fire department was there by the time I got Duncan out, and they took us both to the hospital. The cops asked me all kinds of questions, but because the newspapers snapped a picture of me carrying my brother and ran it on the front page they didn't ask 'em very hard, if you know what I mean. Mom was all mad at me, told me it was *my* fault that her baby'd come so close to dying..." My eyes teared up again. "...and then, that was when the bad stuff *really* started happening."

Forster's jaw dropped. "I... I mean..."

I grinned again. "How can it get any worse? Use your imagination, Doc! Duncan was *all* messed up; when they finally let him out of the hospital he had clubs for feet and claws for hands and no lips... He was blind, too, so he couldn't take care of himself at all. And Mom... She was a druggy. Guess what happened to his pain pills?"

My therapist sat silent, mouth still agape, beyond shock. It was probably unprofessional, but who could blame him?

"Anyway... He didn't get his pills, so he'd scream and gurgle and drool all over the place. Then Mom'd get mad and hit him to make him shut up and take care of hisself better, and he'd just scream louder. We didn't have anything, not even enough to eat, because no one wanted to come and lie with Mom while a burned child was screaming in the next room. At first I tried to take care of him, as best I could. But..." My face screwed up again. "But..."

Forster leaned forward. "Jesus, Cheetah!" he said, reaching out to touch my shoulder. "You were just a child yourself. And... What a nightmare!"

"It was a nightmare, all right," I agreed, no longer weeping. On this part, at least, I was long-since cried out. "The worst nightmare I hope I'll ever know." I looked down at my feet again. "They took Duncan away eventually, and me too. He died in a hospital room, alone, screaming to the very end. It was skin-graft infections that got him, something that didn't ever need to happen if I'd stuck around and taken care of him." I sighed. "But no, I ran away from *that* part of the equation. A few days of him not getting his pills and screaming, and I broke down and was off like a gazelle, sleeping on the streets. There's never been a kid in the universe got a worse deal than Duncan, and a lot of it's my fault. I didn't run away from the fire and I didn't run away the man who set it. But looking at Duncan, all messed up like that day after day after day. . .*That* I ran away from, and because of it he suffered and died. They tried sending me to a foster home, but I tore the crap out of everything they gave me until they finally let me go back to Mom. Where I *deserved* to be. She finally OD'ed while I was in the single-A's; the last time I spoke to her she called me a bastard for getting Duncan killed." I shook my head, then stared down at the desktop for what felt like forever. "So," I said eventually, just to fill the silence like I'd done back when Forster and I had first started, "you can see that I've been square with you, man! I'm *garbage*!" I declared, punching the polished wood surface so hard I thought I'd split it for certain. "Just a pile of useless, worthless garbage that walks around on two legs and never gets nothin' right but messing things up and running away. Even my damn *name* comes from me taking advantage of that poor, innocent little..."

There was another long silence. Presently I wept again. Doctor Forster let me cry alone for a while, then he quietly got up and moved his chair alongside mine. He still didn't touch me, though, for which I was grateful. I didn't want to be touched just then, particularly by a man. "Cheetah?" he said eventually.

I didn't ignore him, exactly. But I was crying so hard that I couldn't do much to respond.

"Cheetah?" he asked again, a little later; this time I was able to turn my head a little. "Can you hear me?"

This time I nodded. "Yeah," I muttered. "I know. We're over time and your associate needs the office, and..."

"No," Doctor Forster replied, his voice low and respectful. "He *doesn't* need this office, Cheetah. Or at least he doesn't need it half as bad as you do, right at the moment at least. You can stay and cry as long as you like—I'd stand off all the legions of hell for you, to give you time to cry. Much less Dr. Lang and his incurable eleven o'clock hypochondriac meal ticket." He sighed. "Cheetah… I'd do *anything* for you." He paused. "*Anything.* Do you know why that is?"

"No," I muttered, still sniffling. "Because you're supposed to do things like that for patients, I guess."

"Heh!" he snorted. "To an extent, yes. But…" His smile faded, and a strange expression spread across his face. It was almost, like, wonder. "In this case, it's something else."

"And what's that?" I demanded, not at all in the mood for games.

"It's because… They say the hottest fires produce the finest steel, Cheetah. And if you aren't the toughest, most remarkable bastard of an upside-down hero that I've ever met in my life, well…" He sighed, then finally laid a hand on my shoulder. Somehow by then it was all right again. "Where you fell short, or fell short in your own mind at least, is merely a reflection of how high you aimed—what an unreachable standard of perfection you demanded of yourself. You've no reason to feel any guilt, son. None at all! No one on god's green earth would hold you responsible for a minute for what happened to Duncan; in fact, just about everyone I know would praise you to the high heavens for dealing with things as well as you did. Compared to most kids, with far more advantages…" He shook his head and scowled. "Well… let's just say that it's been an honor to treat you, though I'd never have guessed that at first. And it's even more of an honor to call you a friend."

"But…" I whispered. "Mom…"

"What was your mother?" he asked, his voice suddenly cold.

"A whore," I answered miserably.

"That's not what I meant," he answered, his voice cold and even. "I meant, what kind of person was she? Be honest, now."

Of their own accord, my fangs suddenly bared themselves.

"Precisely," Dr. Forster said, nodding and smiling again. "You just hold that thought for our next session. I think it'd be a mighty fine place to start, if you feel like it." Then his smile widened. "Now… You've taken a big step today, Cheetah. And it's been hard on you. But not so hard, I hope, that you'll be showing the Muskrats any mercy."

"Heh!" I laughed, this time smiling a little myself. Somehow my heart felt a little lighter than it'd been when I arrived at the clinic that morning. Though why that should be the case beat the heck out of me. And smiling was easier, too.

"You be on your best game, son!" he continued, standing up and reaching out to help me up from my chair. "I'll be three rows back, behind third base. Wearing a spotted hat!"

15

I always arrived at the ballpark a bit late on therapy days, so I missed something really fun. Somehow or another, someone had arranged for Mighty Muskrat to be ready and waiting for our rivals. He was sitting in the visiting coach's office with his feet up on the desk, stuffed with straw and wearing a Catfish baseball cap. Not one but two Catfish pennants were taped to each of his forepaws. Mighty Muskrat was always grinning, but I thought that he seemed even happier and more carefree than usual in his new getup. The Muskrat coach protested that it was an unprofessional and childish prank. Tony absolutely and completely agreed with him between gales of hysterical laughter. So did most of the media, though you'd never know it from all the pictures they took. Somehow they got in a little early as well. . .

I missed most of our last real practice session because it was Cancer Society Day. Coach Turnbull had promised the Belangers that he'd try to get a benefit game scheduled, and he'd made good on his word. He and the front office and I worked out a schedule that, just barely, didn't require me to be in two places at any one point in time. First I showed Raymond and his mom around the stadium a little, which was more of a formality than anything since they'd been there before. Then I spent almost two hours signing autographs. Most minor-league players are required to sign autographs from time to time, because it's every bit as much a necessary professional skill that needs developing as throwing and running and fielding. Coach Turnbull had exempted me from the rotation early-on however, due both to the fur-thing and the fact that I'd already been in the bigs and therefore had some experience. So, this was the Catfish fans' first shot at me. And what a shot it turned out to be! I was entitled to a minimum of twenty bucks a signature, as a former big leaguer. Instead I just put out a big bucket with a sign taped to it that read "Cancer Society Donations" and concentrated on having a good time. It went remarkably well, with none of the snarky fan-comments and innuendos I'd steeled myself to accept. Instead of making sure that everyone paid, I forgot that the bucket was there and focused on smiling and trying to find something pleasant to say to everyone. The ugliest thing that happened was when one middle-aged man commented. "Geez! And the papers all claim you're a jackass! What do they know?" That, and a five-year-old girl became enamored with my tail and yanked on it ruthlessly. It was still a bit sensitive, having just achieved full growth. But I winced and went on like nothing ever happened.

The autograph line was so long that I couldn't possibly get to everyone. When the front-office people finally came to get me so I could begin my warm-ups the queue was nearly as long as it'd been when I started. But they came prepared; by this late in the season the merchandising types had developed a whole line of cheetah-spotted souvenirs, a good number of which I'd signed ahead of time with precisely this situation in mind. These proved to be acceptable substitutes. "Sorry, folks," my suited co-workers explained as I was escorted away, "but there's still a game to be played!" And, miracle of miracles, instead of complaining when I left the crowd *cheered*! "Chee-*tah*!" they roared. "Chee-*tah*! Chee-*tah*! Chee-*tah*!"

Oh, and did I mention that they had to bring a new donation-bucket, too? Three times, in fact.

While I didn't in the least regret doing the autograph-thing, it did have the effect of upsetting my game-day routine. Or at least that's what I blamed for my poor performance in the early innings. I was zip for two at the plate with a walk and got thrown out attempting to steal. Even worse, I made a serious mistake in the field. What should've been an easy ground ball took a bad hop and dribbled through me for a two-base error, allowing a run to score. No one said anything, but everyone knew I was having a bad day. Even young Raymond, whose wheelchair was locked in place right next to my traditional seat at the extreme right-rear corner of the dugout. It was about the safest place to put such a fragile, helpless kid, and though he didn't know it two of us were assigned at all times to make damn sure he didn't get hit by a foul ball or anything like that. "It's all right," he told me when I came in from the field after mishandling the ball, sweat pouring down his face despite the big electric fans we'd set up for his benefit. "Even Ozzie Smith made errors sometimes."

Raymond was always able to put a smiley-face on things; it was a special talent that he had. Somehow, though, I just couldn't. When the bottom of the ninth rolled around we were down 5-2, and suddenly Mighty Muskrat wearing a Catfish hat didn't seem quite so funny anymore. The 'rats were playing like machines; hard, pitiless, and impersonal. We were slowly being crushed in their gears. But there didn't seem to be much hope; the bottom of our order was due up and we'd never gotten a wet firecraker's worth of offense out of them all season long. Even the fans wearing spots were beginning to look tired and sun-wilted.

"It's all right," Raymond repeated, reaching out and laying his skeletal hand on my shoulder. He was a knowledgeable fan for all his youth. Clearly he too knew what time it was. "You guys still had a really good season. Especially you personally, Cheetah." He smiled.

I smiled back, but my heart wasn't in it. Donnie Parker of the double-vision injury, batting seventh, strode up to the plate. He swung at the first pitch, and. . .

. . .miracle of miracles, singled to left field!

"Well!" Raymond observed, sitting up a little higher in his power-chair.

"Yeah," I agreed, as a little ripple of energy surged through the stadium. Now I'd get another at-bat for sure. Not that it'd probably matter. . .

Our next hitter was Hank Greene, a third baseman who really should've been down playing AA ball, and would've been except that our organization was desperately short on talent at his position. I expected Tony to pull him for a pinch hitter, but he didn't. I couldn't help but wonder why. . .

. . .until with two strikes on him, Hank lofted a long fly ball to deep center. It *almost* left the park...

. . .but didn't. Donnie, however, was able to tag up and

advance to second base.

"The pitcher's getting tired," Raymond observed.

"Yep," I agreed. Somehow Tony had seen it where no one else had and held back his pinch-hitter. It'd almost worked, too; another few feet and the ball would've been over the fence. We'd have been one run down with nobody out, and our best batsmen on their way to the plate.

It'd *almost* worked.

The Muskrat bullpen had been intermittently active all afternoon, but now suddenly both a right and left-hander began warming up. Even more significantly, the Muskrat coach came trotting out to the mound to hold a big conference, clearly just wasting time while his relievers loosened up their muscles. "Boo!" the fans began to shout, as the pointless gathering at the mound went on and on. "Boo!" Finally the umps decided enough was enough, applied a little pressure. . .

. . .and the coach pointed to his right arm, indicating he wanted the right-hander. His ace closer.

Reginald Barnes.

The crowd began to boo immediately, and we in the dugout weren't exactly happy to see him either. But, as always, Tony was unflappable. "Pudge," he called out. "You're up."

It was old Pudge Jefferson he was referring to, of course, as Pudge Hiller was already in the game. "Right," the gray-haired old veteran agreed. He stood up and stretched, his long-abused body, joints creaking and snapping. Then he smiled, something we almost never saw. "I guess this'll be my last at-bat. Ever."

"I reckon so," Tony agreed. Then he smiled, too.

Gradually, not all at once, the crowd figured it out as well. Pudge Jefferson had a long and distinguished career behind him, and in his day had been one of the more admired figures in the game. An era was ending, and to mark it the fans slowly came to their feet. "Pudge! Pudge! Pudge!" they chanted, creating a sincere if pale echo of the elderly catcher's glorious past. "Pudge, Pudge, Pudge!" And, for the only time that I knew of in his entire career, Pudge tipped his hat to the crowd in acknowledgement as he stepped up to the plate.

They went wild!

Our backup catcher was a real earthmover in the batter's box; it took him perhaps thirty seconds to shuffle around enough dirt to make him happy. Then he raised his bat and waited, the very picture of a calm, cool professional.

Out at the mound, Barnes shook off first one pitch, then another. There was a scar on his left cheek, still a little puffy. You'd never know to look at either of them that the batter he was facing was the man who'd put it there. Finally he wound up, kicked, and delivered. . .

. . .a vicious, sizzling fastball way close inside! A brushback! Pudge leapt back from the plate. . .

. . .and suddenly the chant of "Pudge! Pudge! Pudge!" turned into an angry mutter.

"Time!" the ump called. Then he jogged out to the mound to have a little discussion with Mr. Barnes.

"Jeez!" Raymond declared. "I mean. . . Wow! I've never seen *anything* like this!"

"That's why they call it hardball, kid," I muttered, grabbing my bat and heading for the on-deck circle. I really should've been out there already, but had waited in order to allow Pudge to have his last moment of glory to himself.

"I'll see you after you cross home plate!" Raymond declared, his voice as angry as mine.

Presently the ump returned to his position behind the catcher, Pudge stepped back into the batter's box and did his landscaping routine all over again, then the pitcher toed the rubber. This time, the pitch came hard, fast and straight right down the middle. An arrogant challenge, to which Pudge didn't rise. The count was now one ball and one strike.

I frowned slightly. Clearly, friend Reginald had his stuff today. This was not a Good Thing.

Then he delivered again. This time Pudge swung. There was a penetrating "crack" as lumber met horsehide. . .

. . .and there was never a second of doubt. The ball was gone,

gone, gone!

The crowd screamed, yelled, even danced in the aisles as Pudge Jefferson solemnly trotted the basepads, moving not much more slowly than what for him would've been a flat-out sprint with his gimpy used-up legs. Then he tipped his hat again, stepped on home plate, and ended a fine career with class and panache despite Reginald's best effort to spoil it all for him.

The score was now 5-4, with one out. There was nobody on, and now it was my turn to face Mr. Barnes.

16

Baseball is a team sport. They drill that into your head over and over again, the coaches do, when it's time to share credit for a victory or hone group-skills like double-play combinations. But it's also very much an individual game as well. When a man stands at the plate, no one else stands there with him. I was a team player these days, more so than I'd ever been in my career. Yet I was also still very much who I'd always been, deep down, and if I were to claim that I didn't relish every nanosecond of these one-on-one encounters I'd be lying through my fangs.

Where Pudge was an earthmover, I normally took a pretty straightforward approach at the plate. A couple of kicks at the ground, one or two steadying swings, and I was ready. But, just this once. . . I aped every motion that Pudge had made, hoping that it'd irritate poor young Reginald to death. Then, just as he seemed almost ready to deliver the first pitch I called time. "What's wrong?" the ump demanded.

"I've got something in my eye!" I complained.

They sent out Herman, who was intelligent enough to thoroughly work me over even though he must've known that I was faking it. Then he dabbed at me one last time and I returned to the batter's box and repeated Pudge's landscaping performance. At the last possible second I reached up and scratched my nose with my middle finger, just as I had the day Reggie and I had first met. This time, his face remained impassive. He shook off a pitch, then performed his beautiful windup. . .

. . .and brushed me back from the plate, just as he had Pudge a few minutes before. The pitch was so far inside that I had to drop to the ground to avoid it.

"Time!" I called again, and the ump nodded. It was a reasonable enough request after a brushback. I shook the dirt off my uniform as best I could, while the crowd muttered and complained. Then I patted down my fur, stepped back into the box, and scratched my nose with my middle finger again.

There are three ways to deal with being brushed back at the plate. One is to accept the rebuke and stand a little further away. Or one could do as Pudge had just done—pretend the unpleasant event had never happened and stand right in exactly the same spot.

But me being me, I crowded the plate even tighter.

Reginald scowled, then wound up and delivered. The pitch was low, almost in the dirt. "Ball two!" the ump declared.

I had a real advantage going for me now, with a 2-0 count. I stepped back out of the batter's box, took a couple steadying swings, then eased back in. Reginald shook off a pitch. . .

. . .and something went 'click' in my mind. He'd thrown two brushbacks already, and both of them had followed shake-offs. Well, I knew what to do about *that*.I gritted my teeth...

. . .then involuntarily flinched anyway as the bastard threw a hundred-mile-an-hour fastball directly at my legs. He was willing to let me have a base, it seemed—so long as I was too crippled to run once I got there! I skipped the rope, just like I'd done dozens of times before in my baseball career. But there was something different this time. I thought I was clear. . .

. . .then something yanked at my spine, and my tender, newly-grown tail was in absolute agony!

"Crap!" I cried, collapsing to the ground in pain. "You jackass! I think you *broke* it!" Herman came running out with his ice pack, and while he looked me over I realized dully that a crowd was forming around home plate.

"You aren't going to give him a base for *that*, are you?" demanded the Muskrat coach.

"I. . ." the umpire stuttered. "I. . ."

"If he hadn't gone and altered hisself," he continued, "he wouldn't even *have* a tail! Now would he?"

"It's an unfair advantage!" the Muskrat catcher, whom I'd once so viciously spiked, added sincerely.

"Uh. . ." the umpire declared.

"What kind of crap is *this*?" Tony countered, jogging up angrily. "My man here's been hit by a pitch. Everyone in the place saw it! And once he's able I assume he'll be on his way to first base! It says right in the rule book that when a batter is hit by a pitch, he's to be awarded first base!"

"Uh. . ." the ump repeated, looking very lost.

"But," the Muskrat's leader countered, "when that rule book was written batters didn't have tails, now did they? None of them! So, some of them didn't have an unfair advantage over others!"

"Aw, come off it!" Tony countered. "Pudge Hiller is twice Cheetah's size! If Cheetah gained a hundred pounds and got hit in the belly, he'd be awarded the base and you wouldn't have a single word to say about it. Or, say, if he'd stretched out his earlobes all long and dangly to wear jewelry, like some of the Carribbean players do these days? Getting hit *there* would have to count, wouldn't it? Or. . . what if his ankle was swollen, and he was barely brushed? Or if he wore shoes a size too big?"

"Uh. . ." the ump stuttered.

"And I suppose that if I had my fielders grow hands the size of watermelons you wouldn't object to that, either!" the Muskrat snapped back. "Baseball players are supposed to be *human*!"

"What *is* 'human', anyway?" Tony demanded, kicking up a cloud of dirt. "Can *you* define it?"

"You're kidding!" his Muskrat counterpart declared, ripping his hat off of his head and using it to point at my now obviously-fractured tail. "Are you going to claim that anyone with one of those things growing out of his butt is still entirely human?"

"Immanuel Kant claimed that humanity is an end, not a means," opined the Muskrat catcher.

"You shut your trap!" his coach raged, pointing an angry finger at his player. "Right now!"

"The Objectivists think that a human is a being that can operate at the conceptual level," Herman declared as he expertly taped up my tail. It was amazing to watch; you might've imagined he'd done it a hundred times before. "Or at least that's how *I* understand their philosophy. But Plato defined man as a featherless biped." He shrugged. "Take your pick. I find them both pretty useless here and now."

The Muskrat catcher's eyes narrowed behind his mask. "I prefer the Turing test, myself."

"I told you to shut up!" the Muskrat coach exploded. Then he turned to Tony. "Never sign a catcher with brains! He'll be the biggest pain in the behind you've ever dealt with."

"Maybe," Tony growled, eyeing me. "And maybe not."

"Crap!" the umpire finally declared, removing his mask and wiping his brow. "How come I've never got a dictionary on me when I really need it?" Then he turned to the catcher. "I think that it's pretty much impossible to assign a meaningful definition to the term 'human' in the absence of a godhead and/or divine revelation on the subject. We can't comprehend our own true natures, you see, any more than a kettle can contain itself." The man in blue blinked. "But, what's a Turing test, anyway? I've never heard of it."

The catcher smiled, and his eyes lit up. "It's where you take—"

"Jesus God almighty!" the Muskrat leader interrupted, raising his eyes to the heavens. "What did I ever do to deserve this?"

***

The ump finally did award me first, on the basis that it might be an affront to our Maker to deem me non-human and therefore a nonplayer. "Only God can properly define humanity," the umpire humbly explained to the two coaches. "And therefore only God can determine if an animal tail grafted onto one of His children becomes a human tail and thus a legitimate part of a ballplayer. It's not my place as a mere mortal to define a tail directed by a human soul as *non*human, in other words. So the batter gets first base. Play ball!"

"Damn!" the other manager cursed, removing his hat again and stomping it into the earth. Then he kicked up an enormous cloud of dust.

"That's no way to pass a Turing test," Herman pointed out as he gathered up his gear and sent me trotting off to first.

"Go to hell, you little twerp!" the manager roared.

The ump promptly fined him fifty dollars for unsportsmanlike behavior. "If you can't find it within yourself to operate at the objective level," he warned, "you can watch the rest of the game from inside the clubhouse! It don't matter none to me!"

First base was a *much* calmer place than home plate, I decided once I got there. Or at least to begin with it was. My tail was throbbing, but I tried to shut the pain out. "A featherless biped?" the first baseman asked me when I arrived.

"Apparently so," I agreed, not much in the mood for conversation. "But only if it's a featherless biped that's an end, not a means."

"Heh!" the Muskrat chuckled. Then Barnes toed the rubber, and it was back to business again. I touched the bag ever-so-gently with my toe, and the contest began. Reginald watched closely as I edged away from the base. . .

. . .then spun and threw to first as I danced back in standing up. It was just like spring training; neither of us had revealed anything like our best. Then we repeated the whole sequence all over again; he threw a second time and I danced back in safe by an easy margin.

"At least I know he loves me," I pointed out to the first baseman, who seemed a nice enough guy. For a Muskrat, at least.

"Heh!" he laughed, throwing the ball back to the mound.

Reginald's next throw was to home plate. Thumps took the pitch. "Ball one!" shouted the ump, and I grinned a little.

"Kid's come a long way," the first-bagger observed as his catcher made a trip out to the mound to talk things over. "You should be proud."

I blinked, then looked the Muskrat in the eye to see if he was kidding. "How. . . I mean. . ."

"Everyone knows you're mentoring him," he explained. "Kid's proud as can be of it."

"I. . . I mean. . ." I stuttered. But before I could say anything more the catcher trotted back home. My eyes narrowed. He was a brainy one, that catcher. Had a good head on his shoulders. And that little conference. . .

I stood up straight and tall at first base and placed both hands firmly on my hips. It looked natural as could be, but it was a signal. "I'm not stealing at this time," it meant. Making the attempt right then just felt like a Really Bad Idea, sort of. Buster could've over-ruled me, but he must have detected something fishy in the air as well. So he acknowledged instead, then repeated the signal to Thumps at the plate. That way the kid could concentrate on nothing but his own at-bat.

Reginald, of course, had no way of knowing I wasn't going anywhere. So we danced again, he and I, and this time even though I had no intention of stealing I wandered just a tiny bit further from the base. That way he wouldn't be able to forget me. Now I had to dive back in when he threw, making things *much* closer. Once I landed wrong on my broken tail and it hurt like hell. "Owww!" I cried out, calling time and staggering around the bag. Herman trotted out with his kit, but I waved him back. The umpires were prepared to cut a certain amount of slack for a player who'd just been hit by a fastball, but I'd be forced to leave the game if the trainer came out to see me many *too* many times. And how could I face Raymond then?

"That thing broken?" the first baseman asked sympathetically.

Once again, I smelled rotten fish. If I let him know where I was vulnerable. . . "Just bruised a little," I lied. "I jarred my head, mostly. It's still tender from the fractured-skull thing."

"Oh," the Muskrat replied, smiling what I now understood was a very false smile. Sure enough, when the next toss from the mound arrived, he tagged me right on the butt. Hard! It hurt even worse than my broken head had, and had to have been deliberate because it wasn't anything like the most convenient place for him.

I got up and made a great show of patting the dust out of my fur, face impassive all the while. Then, just to drive the point home, I gritted my teeth and forced myself to thoroughly pat it out of my tail as well, just exactly as I might've if everything was perfectly fine and dandy and it didn't feel like I was dipping the broken area into molten metal. The Muskrat looked disappointed.

"Play ball!" the ump directed.

This time I leaned a little further towards second, trying to make it look like I was going even though my lead was a bit shorter than usual. Sure enough, Reginald took the bait! Instead of delivering a normal pitch he threw a bullet a good three feet outside, which the catcher fielded standing up and ready to throw to second. A pitchout! But the whole thing was wasted because I hadn't tried to steal in the first place. What a tragedy!

"Ball two!"

Now things were really getting interesting. Thumps had run up a count of two balls and no strikes, which put him well ahead of the pitcher. He could afford to take questionable pitches now and try to draw a walk. Or, alternatively, he could reach out and swing at a bad pitch just to get in the way and obstruct things a little while I stole second. It was no surprise to me at all when the catcher jogged back to the mound. *What are they going to do?* I asked myself. *What looks, to them, like the surest way to shut us down?* Then I frowned, looked down at my feet. . .

. . .and stood straight and tall once again, both hands on my hips. This time, Buster was already giving me the same sign, *telling* me not to try and steal. We'd obviously both come to the same conclusion; they were convinced that I was going to run, because after all that was just what I did, what my whole hyper-aggressive image as a ballplayer was all about. So the pitchout was on again, and to heck with the ball and strike count. I wanted to grin at Buster and say something like "Great minds think alike, eh?" But, of course, there was no chance of *that* happening.

This time, they didn't try to hold me close at all. Or at least not very close. *Come in to my parlor, said the spider to the fly. . .*

. . .and once again I stood safe at first base while Barnes and his catcher executed a textbook-perfect pitchout. They'd have nailed me for certain, had I fallen for it.

"Ball three!" the ump intoned.

This time, the coach came out to the mound to hold one of his famous conferences. Buster came trotting over from his third-base coaching box with a big smile on his face. "You're doing great, kid!" he assured me.

"Well enough," I agreed. "For still being stuck at first." Then I scowled out at the big pow-wow on the mound. "They're going to walk Thumps intentionally," I predicted. "And bank on the double-play."

"It's what I'd do," Buster agreed. Then he grinned. "You could score on a fly ball from third. If you were on third, that is. I mean, you'd have to figure out a way to get there, first. . ."

I grinned back. "I would, wouldn't I?"

Wordlessly he clapped me on the shoulder and trotted away.

17

Dancer, in my opinion, was the most underestimated man on the entire Catfish roster. Because he was so very gay, because he so often wore such a silly grin, because he crossed his legs while standing in the outfield, well. . . People tended to overlook his talents. But even more they overlooked the hard-as-nails grit that lay just beneath the surface. If someone were to ask the Muskrats who the toughest, meanest Catfish was, they might've named Pudge Hiller or Pudge Jefferson. Or they might even have pointed at me. But Dancer routinely played with injuries far more severe than anyone else did, was batting just over .300, and had stolen enough bases to be leading most teams in the category. He was a star in his own right, by AAA standards at least. But while I filled up the stands with cheetah-spotted hats and Pudge Hiller's towering home runs often led the local news, no one ever seemed to notice when Dancer drove in the game-winning RBI, or scored from second where a lesser player would've been thrown out. Dancer, in short, didn't get any respect. Or at least he didn't get any respect outside our clubhouse—*we* appreciated the heck out of him and he knew it. I asked him how he felt about it once, when the spotted-hat phenomenon was first taking off.

"Oh, come *on*, Cheetah!" he countered, when I pointed out that his stats weren't any worse than mine overall. "What are the fans supposed to do to support me? Show up in pink tights?"

He had a point, I was forced to admit. But it still never seemed quite fair to me that he didn't get the credit he deserved. Now here he was at the plate, with the game-winning runs on base and the entire season at stake.

It's a lot harder for a pitcher to hold a runner close at second than it is at first, for several reasons. One is simple geometry; turning a hundred and eighty degrees isn't as easy as pivoting a mere ninety. Also, the shortstop and second-basemen are the keystones of the infield's defensive structure. Moving either one out of position to cover the bag upsets everything else. But perhaps the biggest reason why pitchers have trouble covering second is that they don't get nearly as much practice. Few baserunners are willing to risk stealing third. A player at second is already in reasonable scoring position; most won't accept the risk of being thrown out merely to improve their situation slightly.

I wasn't most baserunners, however, and neither was Thumps behind me. We executed a perfect double-steal right under Barnes' nose, on the very first pitch. Now there were *two* runners in scoring position, and the heat was *really* on!

I didn't envy the Muskrat coach just then; he had some very difficult decisions to make. Barnes was his ace reliever; in fact, he was his *only* quality short-man. So if he pulled him, who else could he go to? And, despite the fact that he was in so much trouble, Barnes was performing fairly well overall. The only hit he'd given up was that one home run to Pudge Jefferson. Other than that, no one else had even laid wood on the ball. Even Thumps' walk had been intentional. The Muskrat's leader had to consider the bigger picture, too. It wasn't his job to win this particular game so much as to develop stars for his parent organization. If Reginald Barnes went on to a major-league career, as even I was forced to acknowledge that he almost certainly someday would do, he'd need all the self-confidence he could get. And what kind of confidence-builder would it be for Barnes if his coach pulled him now, when he was arguably doing so well? I could almost hear the gears grinding over in the Muskrat dugout. But in the end Barnes stayed.

Dancer had swung at the first pitch to help us steal. The next pitch evened the count to a ball and a strike, then the third was a called strike. Dancer called time, stepped out of the batter's box, and proceeded to knock the dirt out of his spikes. He was well behind on the count but seemed undaunted. Meanwhile the crowd had gone silent.

Reginald coiled himself up, unwound, and delivered in his always-elegant motion. The ball sizzled to the plate. Dancer didn't bat an eye; he'd been taking all the way. "Ball two!" the ump intoned.

Barnes scowled, and before throwing the ball back to the mound the Muskrat catcher turned and looked wordlessly at the ump. The pitch had just missed the high outside corner. Or perhaps it hadn't missed the strike zone at all and the ump called it wrong. That was part of the game, something that one learned to live with.

Or perhaps *didn't* learn to live with, in young Reginald's case. When the ball came back to him he stepped off the rubber and then savagely slammed it into his glove, frowning mightily.

Meanwhile Dancer was examining Reggie very closely indeed. When the next pitch came he took it again. "Ball three!" the ump declared, though once again it was a very questionable call.

"Aw come on!" the Muskrat catcher protested. "That caught the corner!" But the ump stood impassive, daring the player to push the argument any further. Wisely, he didn't.

Once again Reginald slammed the ball over and over into his glove, his loss of composure clear for all to see. The proper move would've been for the coach to come out and calm him down, but that wasn't possible because the rules stated that if he went out to visit the mound twice the pitcher had to be replaced. So instead the catcher did his best to fill the void. He returned to the mound and had a long heart-to-heart with his young partner. When it was over Reginald seemed a little more relaxed. On the outside, at least.

The next pitch was a foul ball, a line shot just wide of third that passed so close to me I could hear it hiss angrily through the air. Had it the thing been hit two inches to the right it would've been a game-winning triple.

The ump examined the ball when it came back in and decided it was too badly scuffed to be used any further. So he pulled another from his seemingly-infinite supply and handed it to the catcher. "Play ball!" he urged.

Barnes nodded and caught the new ball. He was visibly upset again, having just come within a whisker of losing the biggest game of his career to date on the last pitch, and to a notorious faggot at that. Finally he toed the rubber, wound up, delivered. . .

. . .and threw the ball all the way to the backstop! Instinctively I ran two steps, then held up when I remembered that this was ball four. Dancer had walked, was all; it didn't count as a passed ball or wild pitch.

"Take your base," the ump declared.

And you damn well earned it! I didn't add, though I smiled and nodded when Dancer's eye caught my own. He was all excited and sparkly, like a big overgrown kid. He always got that way when he thought he'd made someone he didn't like look really bad.

Now the bases were loaded and Pudge Hiller was stepping up to the plate. *Folks,* I could almost hear the radio announcer saying, *It doesn't get any better than this!*

***

I expected to see a reliever when Pudge came to the plate, and probably so did most of the folks in the stands. Even Reginald himself expected to be relieved, I could tell from the way he kept glancing over towards his dugout. But no new hurler was forthcoming, and gradually it began to penetrate that there was going to be no rescue, that he was going to be left to sink or swim on his own. Barnes gulped visibly, then turned to face the huge Pudge Hiller, who was already standing in the box and waiting.

The very same man he'd beaned so viciously, last time he'd faced him.

Pudge had been an amiable, happy sort of man right up until his marriage went sour. Things had changed considerably since then, however, and the changes were accompanied by a surge in his stats. Where once he'd kept himself shaved clean, now a rough, unkempt beard grew in ugly patches all over his face. He was working out more, increasing his already impressive bulk. And even I couldn't meet his angry eyes for long.

Our catcher swung at the first pitch so hard that the sound was audible all over the stadium—*wooof!* It was a titanic swing, the stuff of pitcher's nightmares.

"Strike one!" the ump declared.

Reginald was sweating heavily now; in fact, the stuff was pouring off of him. He shook off a pitch, and I wished there was a signal that'd let me warn Pudge he was about to be brushed back. The ball was way inside when it arrived. . .

. . .but Pudge didn't flinch a millimeter from the deadly missile, even though it barely missed him. Instead he just dug in deeper and grinned. The expression was neither pretty nor meant to be.

"Ball one!"

The catcher returned the ball to the mound. Then Reginald took a little break to finger his rosin bag. After that he paced around a little, still sweating furiously. Meanwhile Pudge simply stood and waited, patient as a mountain. Or a tombstone.

Reginald glanced towards the dugout again, his eyes appealing for mercy. But no rescuer emerged. *This is what happens,* I noted to myself, *on the day when one's chickens finally come home to roost. And when a coach decides it's time for the really hard lessons to be learned.* Finally, Barnes sighed and climbed back onto the rubber. Then, in his always-beautiful style he came to the set position, wound up and delivered a white-hot fastball to the low outside corner.

"Ball two!" the ump ruled.

"Aw, come on!" Reginald cried out from the mound. "Are you blind and stupid *both*?"

"Ball two!" the ump repeated, a hint of belligerence edging its way into his voice.

Reginald scowled, and for just a moment I thought that he was going to resolve his difficulties by getting himself thrown out of the game. The way that I myself might've, once upon a time. But, just barely, he bit off the smart-aleck remark he was about to make and went to his rosin bag instead.

I glanced over at the first base coach. He was fanning himself with his hat, looking for all the world like a sweaty middle-aged man with too much belly seeking a little relief from the heat. But I knew better, as did everyone else out on the basepads. Dancer acknowledged the signal by kicking first base twice, then Thumps and I did the same at our own bags. Unable to help myself, I smiled up at the sky where no one could see it. *Boy,* was young Reginald in for a surprise! Especially since the count and other factors were, in theory, all wrong for what we were about to attempt. No sane coach would *ever* call such a play, in fact. . .

. . .unless he had three speedsters on base whose running skills he trusted heart and soul.

None of us had been leading off much because there wasn't anyplace for anyone to go. The only base available to be stolen was home plate itself, and to his credit once or twice Reginald had thrown to the third baseman to hold me close, just in case I actually *was* insane enough to make the attempt with our finest batsman at the plate, the bases loaded and only one out. Now all three of us edged a little further away from our bags—not enough so as to be conspicuous, but plenty to make a difference when play began. Reginald took a good long look at me, then decided once again that I wasn't that nuts after all. He wound up, kicked, and fired a slider right down the middle. Pudge grinned like a savage, but then instead of swinging with all he had. . .

. . .he squared around to bunt!

I was already a quarter of the way home when the ball struck Pudge's bat and dribbled directly towards me, right down the baseline itself. For a brief but crucial instant not a single Muskrat moved; none of them could comprehend that such a dangerous, even notorious power-hitter might do such a thing. I'd taken three long steps before the catcher rose, pivoted and shifted his position to block home plate. He placed himself well, so well that I for an instant I doubted that I was going to make it.

But it was far too late to worry about *that*! What was going to happen was going to happen. Carefully I skipped over the slowly-rolling ball—if I'd touched it I'd have been called out. This threw me off stride a bit, so I wasn't quite at full speed as I powered the rest of the way down the line, legs driving, heart pumping, face a ferocious fanged snarl. Meanwhile a sort of blur passed close behind me; Reginald on his way to field the bunt. I timed things carefully, leapt face forward as hard as I could. . .

. . .and watched with relief as first the catcher's eyes widened, then he leapt to his feet to shag Reginald's off-balance, thoroughly rattled and too-high throw!

I *could've* hurt the catcher and gotten away with it, just like the first basemen had deliberately tried to hurt me. Instead I slid into home like a gentleman, reaching between the catcher's legs to touch home plate a good hundredth of a second before he tagged my helmet.

"Safe!" the ump cried out. The tying run was home, but play was still underway. Hoping to salvage at least *something* out of the debacle the catcher threw the ball towards first, where Pudge was still charging up the baseline just as quickly as he could. He'd have been thrown out, too. . .

. . .except that the first baseman, as stunned as everyone else, fumbled the ball! It went rolling out into right field!

"Come on!" I urged Thumps, springing to my feet and waving my arm in the big circle that's the universal signal for "keep going!" "Come on!"

Thumps had quite correctly slid into third; now he had to get back on his feet and pick up momentum from scratch. No one else in baseball, I sincerely believed, not even at the pro level, could've come sprinting down the baseline like he did after such a disadvantageous start. Apparently the Muskrat right-fielder had a cannon for a throwing arm; he threw well over the cutoff man's head and directly to home, where the catcher was now waiting for a *second* play at the plate. The ball came racing in, Thumps gave it all he had. . .

. . .then there was a cloud of dust at the plate and a long, long silence. "Safe!" the ump finally declared. "The runner is *safe!*"

18

No one spends a lot of money on security at a minor-league ballpark. Sure, there's a few guards around to eject drunks and things like that. But AAA ballparks are normally a sleepy, placid sort of place. You don't even expect to see a lot of enthusiasm expressed there, much less a riot. Not even on the day that the home team wins their division.

But a riot is exactly what erupted.

It wasn't nearly as bad as it might've been, at least compared to what sometimes happens after big-league victories. No one turned over police cars or looted the souvenir stands or assaulted us players or anything like that. In fact, I never for second felt like I was in any danger when the crowd mobbed the field. They were happy, was all, not angry and drunk and vile and eager to make a name for themselves by hurting someone famous. In fact, the only pain or inconvenience they caused me at all was when they lifted me and Thumps up on their shoulders and paraded us around the infield. That hurt my freshly-broken tail some, sure enough. But was I going to complain? Not hardly! Especially not after I looked down and saw that one of the fans carrying me and cheering his lungs out was my therapist, Dr. Forster.

Eventually the crowd deposited us safely in front of the dugout, where a second independent riot had broken out. We might've been minor leaguers, but we sure as heck knew how to pop a champagne cork and spray each other down well enough! The stuff made my fur a sticky mess and tickled something awful in my ears. It wasn't, however, anything that couldn't be fixed by being thrown time and again into an ice-cold shower while still fully dressed. The best part of all might've been watching Raymond sit in the corner in his power-chair, drinking it all in with hungry eyes. He might not have time to accumulate many memories, I figured. But at least we'd seen to it that some of them were *good* ones.

When things finally began to wind down a little I noticed a

figure standing next to Raymond. He was long-boned and lean, just like I was, and had the same hungry look in his eyes. It was Mr. Sandrell, the team's owner, who none of us had even realized was in the ballpark. I smiled in genuine pleasure and strode across the wet, sticky floor to greet him. "It's just like you, sir," I said, removing my cap, "To come to the game and sit in an ordinary seat, that is."

He grinned. "Fourth row, center-field bleachers," he admitted. "Sometimes I *do* use my personal box, of course. But games often have more flavor when enjoyed from the stands. And you meet the most *wonderful* people!"

I grinned, understanding exactly what he meant. "Well," I said. "Congratulations, sir. I know it's not much of a championship. But such as it is, it's yours."

Sandrell grinned, then extended a hand for me to shake. "It's *ours*, Cheetah. *Ours*." Then the smile faded. "We came in fifth in the bigs. Next year *will* be better." He cocked his head to one side. "Plan to start the season there. You and Pudge both. Probably Dancer, too."

I gulped. "What about Thumps?"

The team's owner frowned. "It could happen," he allowed. "Though I suspect another season down here would do him good. He still needs to grow up a little."

I nodded. "You're probably right. But know this. When he *does* grow up he's going to be a superstar. One of the finest ever to play the game. Anything I can do, he'll soon do better."

Sandrell's eyes narrowed again, then he smiled. "You've grown up a lot yourself," he observed.

I felt myself blush under the spotted fur. "Maybe," I allowed.

"Heh!" the older man chuckled. "I've been keeping tabs on you, son. Better ones than you probably realize. I know what you've done this year, not just for yourself but for Thumps and Pudge and some others, as well." He smiled again. "You may be right, Cheetah, about Thumps outperforming you someday. But he'll never be more valuable or beloved in my clubhouse. Never!" He placed his hand on my shoulder. "No one will be, so long as you continue to walk the straight and narrow. Because you have *other* talents, young man, which you've barely begun to explore. You may not even realize you have them yet, or how rare they are. But they're very much in evidence." Sandrell's smile faded. "What are your plans for the off-season?"

I shrugged. "To tell you the truth, I haven't had much time to think about it."

He nodded. "I own two winter-league teams, Cheetah. They're bottom of the barrel so far as prestige goes; kids just out of high school, mostly. The rawest of the raw recruits. I'd never ask you to *play* at such a low level—it's not worth the risk of you being injured, among other things. But... Have you ever considered coaching?"

My mouth opened, but no words emerged.

"You don't have to decide tonight," he continued, ignoring my speechless state. "Your friend Buster's going to be managing one of them, and he suggested that you might make a fine assistant. The pay won't be much, but you'd be able to stay in shape, keep sharp. . ." His eyes narrowed. "And spend every single day doing what you love most." Then he turned away. "Forgive me. Sometimes I grow jealous."

"Maybe you do, sometimes," I replied. "But you're *always* a gentleman, sir."

"Heh!" he laughed, smiling again. "Ask my ex-wife about that one. Or my other ex-wife!" Then, still smiling, he turned back to Raymond, who'd been taking it all in with wide eyes. "And you," he said. "Don't think that you're getting out of this scot-free, either."

"Huh?" the skinny little boy asked.

"I made a major donation to the Cancer Society today, of course. That was a given. But. . . You know that I own a team in the bigs, right?"

"Uh-huh!" he replied, face a mask of awe.

"And a gengineering company, as well. A rather large one." He smiled again. "I can't make any promises, son, though heaven knows I'd like to. However, I have connections in the industry.

Better ones, I'm certain, than your doctors can dream of. I've already talked to your mother, and tomorrow morning your medical files will be on my desk. They will remain there, the number-one priority of both myself and my staff, every single morning until I find a promising experimental treatment program that will accept you. My sacred word of honor, given to one of the few people I've ever met who loves the game as much as I do."

"Uh. . ." Raymond stuttered.

"In the meantime," he continued, "We owners sort of network together and exchange privileges. Starting next season, show up at any ballpark in the nation and you'll be treated exactly as I would be. Again, my word of honor."

"Gosh!" Raymond gushed. My heart sort of melted, because we all knew the odds were that he wouldn't live long enough to take advantage of Mr. Sandrell's offer. But. . . A man had to do what a man had to do.

Then suddenly Thumps was at my elbow. "Hey, Cheetah!" he greeted me after nodding his respects to Mr. Sandrell. "We're all meeting in the weight room. You're going to be late if you don't hurry."

"Right," the team-owner agreed, eyes twinkling. "Of course." He nodded down towards Raymond. "I'll take charge here. You go to your meeting, Cheetah. And let me know when you've decided about the winter ball thing."

"Sign me up," I declared. "I don't need a lot of time to decide to play ball. And thanks for asking."

Sandrell's eyes twinkled again. "Excellent. Then. . . I suppose I'll be seeing you in the bigs, Cheetah Jones."

19

It was a long walk to the weight room because it'd been added on long after the stadium itself was built. We always held our team meetings there because it was the biggest open space we had. "Cheetah," Thumps said as we strode along. "I want. . . I mean. . ."

I smiled, thinking of poor little Duncan so long ago. For once it didn't hurt. "Yes, Thumps?"

"I. . . Well. . ." he blushed. "I know what you did for me," he said eventually. "And, like. . . Thanks."

"Hah! I had a blast too, Thumps. Someday when we're old we can sit down and laugh again about it."

"I hope so," he said. "I mean. . . Even if we end up on different teams or something, I want you to know that I'll never forget you. And. . . Well, I'd like for us to end up on the *same* team."

I stopped dead in my tracks. "Do you really mean that?" I asked.

"Oh, yes!" he answered, nodding. "Absolutely!"

"Then. . ." I replied slowly. "Well. . . That's the nicest, kindest thing that anyone's ever said to me in my life."

We stood staring at each other for a moment, then Thumps looked down at his feet. "There's something else I want to ask you too," he said finally.

"What's that?" I replied.

He sighed, still staring at his feet. "That fur job. You've got the only one in baseball, and it's sorta like your trademark now." He blushed. "It looks like *so* much fun! It seems to have done you some good, too. And the fans really love it. Would you mind if. . . I mean, I wouldn't do a cheetah. . ."

My jaw dropped, then I slapped my thigh and proceeded to laugh myself silly as Thumps turned redder and redder. "No, I don't mind at all!" I finally managed to spit out. "In fact. . . It just might be good for you, too. Get you out of your own skin, help you loosen up a little."

He nodded, still blushing and staring down at the ground. "Thank you."

"Hah!" I laughed again. Then I grabbed Thumps by the shoulder and sort of steered him down the hall towards the weight room. We were the last to arrive. But it didn't matter. The room was full of happy players, happy coaches, happy trainers, happy front office staff. And up front, sitting happily in the middle of a happy folding table, was the divisional trophy.

"Cheetah! Thumps!" Coach Turnbull greeted us. "Late as usual!" But this time there wasn't a trace of malice in his voice. He turned around, picked up the trophy, and raised it above his head. "This belongs to us all," he explained, and everyone cheered. "To each and every one of us," he continued once the noise died down. "Wherever we go from here, we'll always carry a piece of this trophy, of this victory, of this *fellowship* with us in our hearts. And it's right and proper that this is so." Then he set the big victory cup back on the card table. "But, deep down, I think all of us know that we've earned a greater prize as well. A year here together, sharing the joys and the pains and growing ever closer to one another; that's the true reward." He wiped a tear from his eye. "They call these the minor leagues," he declared, raising his voice like an orator. "But there's nothing minor about any of us, or what we've made happen here together! About who we are, what we've learned, the experiences we've shared, our love for the game. There's nothing minor at all about any of that! Once upon a time, a man condemned to die far too young walked to the middle of Yankee Stadium and declared to a sellout crowd that he was luckiest man on Earth. Well, Lou Gehrig might've been the luckiest way back then; I won't argue with one of the all-time greats about that. But today the honor is all mine."

For a moment silence reigned, then the pandemonium broke out all over again. Half of us were cheering and half of us crying; every few seconds we traded jobs. Then Buster called for attention. "And now," he announced, rolling in a training-table loaded down with smaller trophies, "The moment you've all been waiting for. Individual award time!"

Pudge Hiller won the home-run and RBI trophies, of course, while Dancer earned the overall batting title. Pudge Jefferson took home a special appreciation plaque from all of us players. It was a nice one; everyone put in on it to thank him for sharing his hard-earned wisdom. Thumps won the Biggest Individual Improvement award. . .

. . .and, last of all, I discovered that I'd been elected by my fellow players as the team's Most Valuable Cat.

Who'da ever dreamed it?

OTHER TITLES FROM LEGION PRINTING

By Phil Geusz:

Descent
Lagrange
Left-Handed Sword
Space Man's Burden
Transmutation NOW!
Wine of Battle

The David Birkenhead Series:
Ship's Boy
Midshipman
Lieutenant
Commander
Captain
Commodore
Admiral

The Clan Gonther Cycle
Early Byrd
Fledgeling Byrd
Jail Byrd
War Byrd
Angry Byrd

Written in the Stars
Ursa Major, The Great Bear
Musca, The Fly
Aquarius, The Water Bearer

Edited By Fred Patten

Already Among Us, an Anthropomorphic Anthology

By B. A. Maddux

Lab Rat

By Chris Haggler

Lion Eyes